There was just so much a man could endure before cracking.

"Maybe you'd better go and change," he told her.

Marja raised her eyes to his. "Why?"

Because I'm going to jump you in ten seconds if you don't. "Because I can only be a gentleman for so long." His eyes raked over her body. "And Doc, you're pushing the envelope."

Her breath caught in her throat as excitement and anticipation rushed through her. "What makes you think I don't want that envelope delivered?"

"Careful what you wish for."

As he said the words, Kane could feel the last barrier of restraint shredding.

Dear Reader,

Well, here we are at the end of another miniseries, saying goodbye (worst word in the English language). Marja is the youngest of the Pulaski sisters and she is confident that the happiness her sisters have found is going to elude her, which is all right with her since she loves her family, her career and her lifestyle. Besides, a good man is hard to find—unless, of course, you happen to hit him with your car, which is exactly what happens to Marja. Horrified, she insists on taking care of the man herself, not knowing her life is about to change—drastically. However, not before she learns that things are never exactly what they seem and even the sexiest of men have secrets.

I've had a wonderful time with this series, revisiting the place and, in part, the people I grew up with. And, as for this being the end of the line, well, you never know, there might be a cousin hiding in the wings somewhere, waiting to scrub up.

As ever, I thank you for reading, and from the bottom of my heart, I wish you love.

Love,

Marie Ferrarella

MARIE FERRARELLA

Secret Agent Affair

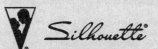

Romantic
SUSPENSE

SILHOUETTE BOOKS

ISBN-13: 978-0-373-27581-6
ISBN-10:   0-373-27581-1

SECRET AGENT AFFAIR

Copyright © 2008 by Marie Rydzynski-Ferrarella

Books by Marie Ferrarella

MARIE FERRARELLA

This *USA TODAY* bestselling and RITA® Award-winning author has written more than one hundred and fifty books for Silhouette, some under the name Marie Nicole. Her romances are beloved by fans worldwide. Check out her Web site, www.marieferrarella.com.

To
Misiu and Marek,
and
growing up in New York City
Love,
Marysia

Chapter 1

She knew better.

Of all people, Dr. Marja Pulaski knew to be alert when she was sitting behind the wheel of a moving vehicle.

It really didn't matter that the vehicle in question, a car she shared with her sister, Tania, was going at a pace that, in comparison, would have made the tortoise of "the Tortoise and the Hare" fame change his name to Lightning. A car was a dangerous weapon, an accident waiting to happen unless it was parked in a garage.

Hadn't she seen more than her share of auto accident victims in the E.R.? Marja was well versed in the kind of damage just the barest distraction could render.

Her excuse, that she'd just come off a grueling double shift at Patience Memorial Hospital, wouldn't have held water with her if someone else had offered it. And everyone knew that the cheerful, outgoing Dr. Marja Pulaski, the youngest of the five Pulaski physicians, was harder on herself than she was on anyone else.

Other than being somewhat vulnerable and all too human, there was no real reason for Marja to have glanced over at the radio just as one of her favorite songs came on. Looking at the radio hadn't made the volume louder, or crisper. And it certainly wouldn't restart the song. It was just an automatic reflex on her part.

The song had been hers and Jack's. Before Jack had decided that he was just too young to settle down, especially with a woman who'd let him know that, although she loved him, she wasn't going to make him the center of her universe.

Trouble was, for a while, Jack *had* been the center of her universe—until she'd forced herself to take stock of the situation and pull back. Pull back and refocus. Being a doctor was not something she knew she could take lightly, especially not after all the effort that had been put forth to get her to that point.

Her parents were naturalized citizens. Both had risked their lives to come to the United States from their native country of Poland. At the time, it was still bowed beneath communist domination. They'd come so that their future children could grow up free to be whatever they wanted to be.

Once those children began coming—five girls in all—the goal of having them all become doctors had somehow materialized. Her father, Josef, and her mother, Magda, worked hard to put their firstborn through medical school. Once Sasha graduated, any money she could spare went toward helping Natalya become a doctor. Natalya, in turn, helped Kady, who then helped Tania. And it all culminated in everyone working together so that she, Marja, could follow in the firm footsteps that her sisters had laid down before her.

She didn't do it because this was the way things were, she did it because, like her sisters before her, she really *wanted* to become a physician. Looking back, Marja couldn't remember a day when she *hadn't* wanted to be a doctor.

But there were moments, like tonight, that got the better of her. She'd spent her time trying to put together the broken pieces of two young souls, barely into their permanent teeth, who'd decided to wipe one another out because one had stepped onto the other one's territory.

So when the song came on, reminding her of more carefree times, she let the memories take over and momentarily distract her.

Just long enough to glance away.

Just long enough to hit whoever she hit.

The weary smile on her lips vanished instantly as the realization of what had just happened broke through. The sickening thud resounded in the August night, causing the pit of her stomach to tighten into a huge, unmanageable knot and making her soul recoil in horror. Perspiration popped out all over her brow, all but pasting her golden-brown hair against her forehead—not because the night air was so damp and clammy with humidity but because the flash of fear had made her sweat.

Her vow, to first do no harm, exploded in her head,

mocking her even before Marja brought the vehicle to a jarring stop, threw open her door and sprang out of her car.

She worked in the city that boasted never to sleep, but at two o'clock in the morning, the number of Manhattan residents milling about on any given block had considerably diminished. When she'd turned down the side street, determined to make better time getting back to the apartment she shared with Tania, her last remaining unmarried sister, there hadn't been a soul in view. Just a few trash cans pockmarking the darkened area and one lone Dumpster in the middle of the block.

You are knowing better than to go down streets like that.

Marja could all but hear her father's heavily Polish-encrusted voice gently reprimanding her. He'd been on the police force over twenty-eight years when he finally retired, much to her mother's relief. Now he was the head of a security company that had once belonged to his best friend and was no less vigilant when it came to the female members of his family.

He was especially so with her because she was the last of his daughters—through no fault of her own, she often pointed out. He always ignored the comment, saying that the fact remained that she was the youngest and as such, in need of guidance. Stubborn mules had nothing on her father.

Marja's legs felt as if they were made out of rubber and her heart pounded harder than a marching band as she rounded her vehicle. She hoped against hope that her ears were playing tricks on her. That the thud she'd both heard and—she swore—felt along every inch of her body was all just a trick being played by her over-tired imagination.

But the moment she approached the front of her car, she knew it wasn't her imagination. Her imagination didn't use the kind of words she heard emerging from just before the front of the grille.

And then the next second, she saw him.

He was lying on the ground. A blond, lean, wiry man wearing a work shirt rolled up at the sleeves and exposing forearms that could have been carved out of granite they looked so hard. The work shirt was unbuttoned. Beneath it was a black T-shirt, adhering to more muscles.

Had the man's shirt and pants been as dark as his T-shirt, she might have missed it. But they weren't. They were both light-colored. Which was how she was able to see the blood.

What had she done?

"Oh God, I'm so sorry," Marja cried, horrified as she crouched down to the man's level to take a closer look. "I didn't see you." The words sounded so lame to her ears.

The man responded with an unintelligible growl and at first she thought he was speaking to her in another language. New York City was every bit as much of a melting pot now as it had been a century ago. The only difference was that now there were different countries sending over their tired, their poor, their huddled masses yearning to be free.

But the next moment she realized that the man spoke English, just growled the words at a lowered decibel. Maybe he was trying to mask the real words out of politeness.

No, she decided in the next moment, he didn't look like the type to tiptoe around that way.

"Are you hurt?"

It was a rhetorical question, but she was flustered. Her parents thought of her as the flighty one, but that description only applied to her social life—post-Jack. Professionally, Marja was completely serious, completely dedicated. She needed one to balance out the other.

"Of course you're hurt," she chided herself for the thoughtless question. "Can you stand?" she asked. Marja held her breath as she waited hopefully for a positive answer.

Rather than reply, the bleeding stranger continued glaring at her. She could almost feel the steely, angry green gaze, as if it were physical.

It wasn't bad enough that he'd just been shot, Kane Donnelly thought. Now they were trying to finish him off with a car.

At least, that was what he'd thought when his body had felt the initial impact of the vehicle's grille against his torso, knocking him down. But now, one look at the woman's face and the sound of her breathless voice told him that she wasn't part of the little scenario that had sent him sprinting down dark alleys, holding on to his wounded side with one hand, his gun with the other.

Damn it, he was supposed to be more on top of his game than this.

Kane swore roundly again. He was a veteran, for God's sake, of the air force as well as the Company. He wasn't supposed to let some barely-shaving punk kid, who hadn't a thing to do with his undercover assignment, get a piece of him as he fired drunkenly into the night.

Taking a deep, ragged breath, Kane began to struggle to his feet, praying fervently to a deity that, until a few minutes ago, he'd firmly believed had left a Gone Fishing sign on His heavenly gate. The prayer encompassed the hope that nothing had been broken in this little-man-versus-machine encounter that had just occurred.

And then, interrupted, he stopped praying.

Kane was surprised that the diminutive woman with the lethal car had begun to prop her shoulder beneath his. Her hands tightened around his torso as she joined him in the effort to make him vertical again.

What the hell was she up to? "Hey," Kane protested angrily.

She didn't let his tone stop her. She was used to being yelled at. It amazed her what people in pain were capable of saying that they'd never even utter under different circumstances.

"Just trying to get you upright," she said in a voice that kindergarten teachers used on their slower students.

Where did she get off, copping an attitude? It annoyed the hell out of him. He needed to be out of here. Needed to see to the bullet wound.

The next minute, as Kane planted his feet on the asphalt a little less firmly than he was happy about, he felt her soft, capable hands traveling up and down the length of his legs.

What the hell was she, a hooker trying to arouse him? Or was she just trying to roll him for money? In either case, he was on his guard. He tried to grab her hands, but she eluded him, continuing to feel up his body.

"Hey," Kane demanded, "what the hell do you think you're doing?"

She would have assumed that would have been obvious, Marja thought. But apparently not to the likes of him. It reminded her just how sheltered, in some ways, she still was.

"Just checking for broken bones. There don't seem to be any," she concluded.

At least, she added silently, no major ones. That didn't mean he didn't have a cracked rib or two. He had blood on his shirt and it had to have come from somewhere. Was it someone else's? The best way to find out just what was going on would be for her to get this man to the hospital.

Straightening, she suddenly saw the reason for the blood. There was a hole in his shirt just beneath the third rib. A hole whose outline was surrounded with blood.

She raised her eyes to his. *That* was why he'd stumbled in front of her car when he had. Why hadn't he said anything?

"You've been shot."

Kane blew out a breath. "No kidding, Sherlock." He bit off the retort. Damn, but the bullet wound hurt like hell. He was pretty sure the bullet was still in there somewhere. This working undercover without benefit of a vest was the pits.

He certainly wasn't in the running for a Mr. Congeniality award, she thought, frowning at him. Marja nodded at the bullet wound. "You need to have that taken care of."

He glanced over his shoulder. No one was coming.

He'd managed to lose the little son of a bitch. Kane looked back at the woman, wondering if he could commandeer her car. "You always state the obvious?"

Definitely not Mr. Congeniality. More in the running for Oscar the Grouch. "Only when I'm talking to a Neanderthal."

She'd give him too much of a hard time if he tried to take her car, he decided, and he was in no condition to take her on. He felt as weak as a wet kitten someone had done their best to drown.

He had to get going before his strength deserted him altogether.

"Well, let's remedy that right now." Kane stepped back, away from the annoying woman, and then turned around on very shaky legs. Right now, he needed to get back to the run-down hotel room his handler had secured for him while he played out this half-assed charade. If he didn't get this bullet out soon, he had the uneasy feeling he was going to pass out.

To his surprise and great annoyance, the woman he was trying to get away from shifted, moving faster than he did. She got in front of him. More than that, she got in his face.

Pointing to his wound, she said, "I can take care of that for you."

Against his will, he winced, the result of taking in a shallow breath. His side felt as if it was on fire. "Haven't you done enough?"

"I'm not the one who shot you," she pointed out. Somewhere in the back of her head, she could envision her father, his frown so deep it imprinted itself into the furrows of his deep jowls, demanding to know what she was possibly thinking, standing and arguing with a man with a gunshot wound. But she couldn't just leave him here. That wasn't why she'd become a doctor.

"Lady, get out of my way," the stranger growled menacingly.

Marja stood her ground on knees that didn't quite feel solid. "I'm a doctor," she told him. "I can take you to the hospital and treat you."

There was disdain on the handsome face. He looked dangerous, she thought, wondering if she was making a fatal mistake.

"Business that slow?"

Rounding the hood, she got over to the passenger side and threw open the door. "Get in," she ordered in the most authoritative voice she could manage. She was channeling her mother, who *no one* disobeyed.

Obviously her future was not in channeling. The stranger didn't move. If anything, his expression grew darker. "No, thanks."

He was about to go. Again, she moved so that she was in front of him, blocking his way out of the side street. He was breathing harder, she noted. It was getting more difficult for him to stand, she guessed.

Marja did her best to brazen him out. "That wasn't an offer you were supposed to refuse."

"I can't go to the hospital." He couldn't afford for his cover to be blown, not when things were beginning to come together, however slowly.

"Why?" Marja demanded.

Even as she asked, she had a feeling she knew.

Anyone who came into the hospital with a gunshot wound had to be reported to the police. The man she'd hit with her car was undoubtedly standing on the wrong side of the law and couldn't risk it. Ordinarily she'd be tempted to back off. But part of this was her fault. She'd hit him with her car and that made her at least partially responsible for this man. Who knew what kind of damage he'd sustained from the impact, however slowly she'd been going?

She couldn't let him just disappear into the night without trying to help. That wasn't the way she had been raised, that wasn't what her Hippocratic oath meant to her.

For one long moment Kane seriously debated just pushing this woman out of his way and making good his getaway.

But despite the fact that there'd been no one to teach him manners, no one to drill the difference between right and wrong into his head, not even when he'd been very, very young, it was second nature to him to rein in the explosive temper that dwelled inside of him. Women were the softer sex and should be treated with a measure of respect—even when they ran you down with their cars.

So rather than become physical, Kane decided to resort to his voice, a voice that had been known to make his handler, a fifteen-year veteran with the Company, cringe and look decidedly uncomfortable. He figured at the very least, that would make the woman back off and leave him alone.

"What the hell do you think you are, lady? My conscience?"

His manner was malevolent, but there was something in his eyes, something that told her she didn't have anything to fear. He wasn't going to hurt her, not for trying to help him at any rate.

"Why?" she asked, her voice mild, curious. "Do you need one?"

His eyebrows narrowed, his eyes looked like thunder. "Get out of my way, lady."

Marja stood her ground and tried again. "I'm a doctor—"

Kane sucked in his breath, struggling to keep the pain at bay. It was distressingly close. "Okay, get out of my way, *Doctor.*"

Marja made a quick decision, not one her parents or her brothers-in-law, all three of whom were in some branch of law enforcement, would have praised, but one she knew she could live with. Hopefully. "If you don't want to go to the hospital, I can still treat you."

She saw suspicion rise into his eyes to replace the darkness.

"And just why would you do that?" Each word was carefully measured out.

"Because I hit you with my car and I owe you one."

Kane found himself leaning against the hood, his knees growing watery. "If you 'owe me one,' get out of my way and we'll call it even."

The infuriating woman moved her head slowly from side to side. A hot breeze moved her hair independently about her face. "Can't do that."

"Sure you can." Getting air into his lungs was becoming difficult. "There's your car." He tried to wave toward it and stopped. The effort to stand grew increasingly difficult. "Get in it, drive away and go hit someone else."

She ignored his protest. "I don't live far from here. I've got everything I need to treat you at my apartment. Please," she pressed, taking a step toward him.

The air turned sweeter. Fruit? Perfume? His brain was scrambled.

"That could get infected."

She was talking about his wound, he thought, his brain oddly feverish. Maybe she had hit him harder than he thought. "And that's your concern how?"

"I'm a doctor," the woman repeated for the third time. She was *really* getting on his nerves.

"You keep saying that," he accused angrily.

To his surprise, he saw her smile. Or was that just a hallucination? "And I'll keep repeating it until you let me treat you."

He knew better, he really did. But he felt dangerously light-headed. Losing all that blood and then getting hit by a car, even if it wasn't going all that fast, had conspired to wreck havoc on his stamina. He began to doubt he could make it back to the hotel room.

And there were cops out. It would be just his luck to attract the attention of one of them. Right now, he wasn't at liberty to explain to one of New York's finest why he was weaving through the streets like a drunken sailor with a gunshot wound.

Like it or not—and he didn't—he was going to have to take a chance on this woman.

"Okay," he growled in his most threatening voice. "But just so you know, I'm armed and dangerous."

Her father had taught her that when she had her back up against a wall, she needed to tough it out and put on the bravest face she could, even if her insides were rapidly turning to jelly.

"Never thought anything else," Marja replied matter-of-factly as she helped the wounded stranger into her car.

He passed out the moment she shut the door.

Chapter 2

Marja drove quickly, squeaking through amber lights about to turn red. She hoped all the police squad cars were in another part of the city. She'd deliberately left the radio off so that she could hear her passenger in case he suddenly came to and said something.

He didn't.

The stranger was still out cold a few minutes later when she pulled into the underground parking garage located directly beneath her apartment building.

Zipping into the assigned parking space, she turned off the engine and eyed the man slumped over beside her.

"Okay, we're here," she announced. There was absolutely no indication that he'd heard her. Nudging him, first gently, then with feeling, accomplished nothing.

Marja placed her fingertips to his throat and felt for his pulse. He was still alive. "Wake up," she ordered loudly.

His eyes remained closed.

Okay, now what? she wondered.

Maybe he'd lost more blood than she'd thought. Marja chewed on her bottom lip, thinking. She needed to get him upstairs. No way could she get him out of the car and into the elevator by herself.

Marja looked at the stranger's face. For a moment she entertained the idea of turning around and driving back to the hospital. Plenty of people could help her there.

But she'd told him that she wouldn't and for some reason she couldn't quite put into words, she felt that it was important that she not lie to the man.

With a sigh, she took out her cell phone. She pressed the keypad for Tania, the only one of her sisters who still lived in the apartment that had originally housed Sasha, Natalya and Kady before all three of them had gotten married. Pretty soon, she knew it would be only her living there. But right now, she shared the three-bedroom apartment with Tania—when her sister wasn't staying over at her fiancé Jesse's place.

The phone on the other end of the line stopped ringing.

"Where the hell are you?" Tania demanded with exasperation the moment she came on. "You were supposed to be here twenty minutes ago. I need the car. They called me in to cover for Michaelson. If I don't get to the hospital in fifteen minutes, I'm going to be late for my shift."

Marja picked her words carefully. She didn't want

to say any more over the phone than she absolutely had to. "I need you to come down, Tania." She glanced toward the slumped figure to her right. "I've, um, got a slight problem."

For a moment there was silence, then anger. "There better be nothing wrong with the car or you're going to be facing more than just a 'slight' problem," Tania warned her.

The next moment the connection was abruptly terminated.

Marja closed her cell phone, pocketing it along with her car keys. Squaring her shoulders, she braced herself for a lecture when Tania arrived. The car was really Tania's, although they did share it. Her sister had bought it from Sasha after their oldest sister had purchased a new one, an SUV to accommodate her family increasing by one. In its time, the vehicle had ferried all five of the Pulaski women to and from the hospital, as well as the house in Queens where they all grew up and where their parents still resided.

Deciding to give it one more try, Marja shook her unconscious passenger's shoulder again and wound up with the same results.

"If you know what's good for you," she murmured to the unconscious stranger, "you'll come to—fast."

The elevator leading up to the other floors was located on the far side of the garage. Marja watched as the doors opened. Her sister had arrived faster than she'd anticipated.

Tania, casually dressed in jeans and a blue pullover sweater, a giant purse slung over her shoulder, quickly cut the distance between the elevator and the parked vehicle to nothing.

It wasn't until she was only about two feet away from her car that she saw Marja wasn't alone in it. And it wasn't until she'd reached the car that she noticed the passenger's condition.

Marja was already out. Rounding the hood, she opened the passenger door. "I need your help to get him upstairs."

Tania stared at her sister, stunned. She was accustomed to Marja bringing men home, but they were usually in a far better state than this one—and conscious. She looked back at the slumped passenger.

"Bringing home hospital overflow, Marysia?" she quipped.

This wasn't the time to get into a discussion. She needed to take care of the stranger's wound before it became infected.

"Just help me get him upstairs, Tania," Marja said wearily. "It's been a long night, not to mention a long day."

Tania made no move to help. Instead she leaned over the passenger side and peered at the man.

"Scruffy, but definitely not bad-looking," she pronounced. Straightening, she glanced at her sister, an incredulous expression on her face. "You were the one who always brought home strays," she recalled. The habit had driven their mother crazy, despite the fact that Magda Pulaski found a way to house each and every wounded animal. "But this—" Tania gestured toward the stranger "—is over the top, even for you."

Marja started to struggle with the man, trying to

move him into position so that they could pull him out of the vehicle. If they both took hold of an arm, they could get him into the elevator.

"I hit him with the car, Tania." It wasn't something she'd wanted to admit, at least not yet. Not until Tania was at least a grandmother. But it was obvious that her sister needed to be coerced.

If she was shocked, Tania didn't show it. Instead she placed her hands on Marja's shoulders and moved her out of the way so that she could get a closer look at the man. After a quick assessment, she raised her eyes to Marja's. "Since when does the car shoot bullets?" she asked. "Sasha never mentioned it could do that little trick."

Annoyed, Marja shifted her out of the way and resumed trying to pull the stranger farther out of the vehicle. "Don't get sarcastic, Tania."

"Don't get stupid, Marja," Tania countered, her arms crossed before her chest. "We're not bringing him upstairs."

"Fine," Marja snapped. She'd finally managed to get him to face out. It was like pushing a rock into position. "I'll do it myself."

Tania watched her continue to struggle for exactly five seconds, muttered a sharp oath and then grabbed the unconscious stranger by the other arm. Marja looked at her in surprise.

"You are the most stubborn woman on the face of the earth," Tania declared angrily. Between the two of them, they hoisted the all but dead weight up to his feet.

"Blame Mama. I got it from her," Marja gasped,

struggling beneath the unconscious man's weight and doing her best not to pitch forward or to fall backward as they slowly made their way to the elevator.

Tania held on to the man's wrist, his arm slung across her shoulders as she took unsteady steps toward the elevator. "You know this is crazy, don't you?"

Marja kept her eyes on the prize, silently counting off steps until they finally reached the steel doors. "We're doctors," she pointed out haltingly.

Leaning her forehead against the wall to help brace herself, Marja pressed for the elevator. When the doors opened almost immediately, she had to keep from falling forward. Breathing a huge sigh of relief—they were halfway there—she punched the button for their floor.

"We're supposed to heal people," she concluded, drawing in a lungful of air as she braced herself for the second half of the journey—getting the man to their apartment once they reached the fifth floor.

Tania craned her neck around the man they held up between them. "That doesn't mean going out and trolling the streets for patients."

"I wasn't trolling. I told you, I hit him with the car."

"How—?"

She'd braced herself for that same question. "One second he wasn't there," Marja answered. "Then he was. And I hit him."

"But you didn't shoot him," Tania insisted. The elevator came to a stop and Tania shifted, getting what she hoped was a better hold on the man. "Why didn't you just take him to P.M. or call the paramedics?"

Holding tightly on to his other hand, lodging her shoulders beneath his arm, Marja began to walk. "Because he wouldn't let me." Why hadn't she ever noticed before how far away their apartment was from the elevator?

Tania glanced at the unconscious face. "Doesn't seem to be putting up much resistance at the moment. The man could be a criminal, you realize that, right?"

Almost there, Marja thought. Almost there. "He's… not."

Tania all but threw herself against the door, then waited as Marja fished out her key. "And you know this how?" she gasped.

Marja didn't answer until she'd managed to unlock the door and resumed her forced march, this time through the doorway. "He doesn't have criminal eyes."

"Right. You're crazy, you know that?"

Marja was getting a second wind. From where, she had no idea. "Whatever you say, Tania. Let's get him… to the sofa," she instructed.

Together, they deposited the man on the sofa. It was hard not to drop him, but they managed. Because of her position, Marja went down with him, then immediately scrambled to her feet.

"I can take it from here," she told Tania, dragging in gulps of air. "You just get to the hospital."

Tania took a step back. She glanced down at her clothes, checking herself over to see if any of the blood had gotten on her. Miraculously, it hadn't.

Losing no time, Marja made her way to the kitchen for some clean towels and a basin of water. "I said you can go," she called. "You don't want to be late," she added.

Tania glanced at her watch. "I'm already late," she

answered, seeming hesitant to leave. Tania shifted un-
comfortably from one foot to the other. "Look, I really
do have to go. I told them I'd fill in for Michaelson,"
she said. "But let me call Jesse." She began to take out
her cell phone. "He can be here in ten minutes and he'll
stay with you until you finish being the Good Samari-
tan."

"No," Marja protested from the kitchen. In less than
a second she was back in the room. Water sloshed out
of the basin as she came. "No, let Jesse sleep," she
insisted, putting the basin down on the coffee table.

The cell phone remained in Tania's hand. She
wasn't going to give up that easily. "All right, I'll call
Byron, then."

That was equally unacceptable. She wasn't about to
put anyone out on her account. Besides, she could take
care of herself. The fact that she was petite and young
had nothing to do with her ability to defend herself if
need be. "No."

"Mike. Tony." Tania offered up the names of their other
two brothers-in-law, both of whom were detectives associated with the N.Y.P.D. Marja firmly shook her head at
the mention of each. Tania frowned. "All right. Dad, then."

Marja's eyes grew huge. "No! Especially not Dad.
You call Dad about this and you're a dead woman."
There wasn't a trace of humor in Marja's voice.

"Better me than you."

"I'll be fine," Marja insisted, depositing the towels
beside the basin. Placing both of her hands to her sister's
back, she steered and then pushed Tania toward the
front door. "Really."

Tania looked far from convinced.

But defeated, she surrendered. Temporarily. "I'm going to call you every fifteen minutes," Tania declared, stepping out into the hallway. "And you'd better answer."

Marja nodded, already retreating into the living room. "I promise." And then she stopped for a second. "And, Tania—"

"What?"

"I'm sorry I hurt the car." There was a dent in the front bumper. It was minor, but there, and she knew how Tania was about her possessions.

Tania waved her hand, dismissing the words. "Yeah, whatever." She looked back into the apartment, at the body on the sofa. "Just be careful."

Marja grinned. "Always."

"Ha!" It was the last word Tania said before she closed the door behind her.

Marja turned her attention back to the unconscious, wounded man on the sofa. Moving quickly, she made her way through two of the bathrooms. Between the two, she collected all the things she was going to need to remove the bullet from his side and then sew up his wound.

As a graduation present, her parents had given each one of them an old-fashioned doctor's black-bag. It was there that she kept the kinds of instruments for digging a bullet out of the man's side. She grabbed hers out of her room.

After depositing everything on the coffee table, Marja pulled on a pair of gloves and got down to business.

They'd dropped him face-down on the sofa. She rolled him over, then pushed open his shirt. Very carefully, she peeled back the T-shirt beneath it. A solid wall of abdominal muscles met her gaze. She hadn't expected that. He looked a little small for a body builder, but perfect enough to be among their number.

"Who *are* you?" she murmured under her breath. Curiosity had her glancing at his left hand. No ring. But that didn't mean there wasn't a wife somewhere, beside herself with worry.

"He's a patient, not a man," she reminded herself. But a torso like that was difficult to ignore.

Taking several cotton swabs, she soaked them in alcohol, then started to clean the area around his wound. The moment she touched the swab to his skin, she saw his muscles contract. The next second he grabbed her wrist. Hard.

It took Marja a full minute to push her pounding heart back out of her throat. Her eyes shifted to his face. He was most definitely awake. And scowling like dark storm clouds over the prairie.

"Welcome back." Marja did her best to sound flippant.

Taking a breath, trying to get his bearings, Kane released the woman's wrist. His eyes moved quickly around the area. It wasn't familiar in the slightest. Where the hell was he?

His eyes shifted back to the woman sitting on the edge of the sofa. There was something white and wet in her hand. "What happened?"

Setting the swab aside, Marja looked at him. She almost wished he was still unconscious. This next part was going to be a lot more painful for him awake. "You fainted."

Kane sneered at the mere suggestion. "Men don't faint."

Oh God, he was one of those. Macho with an extra doze of testosterone. She should have known the second she caught a glimpse of his abdominal muscles. "You passed out," she rephrased, then waited. "Better?"

He shrugged. The movement caused him more than a small amount of discomfort. He felt as if he'd gotten hit by a truck. No, wait, a Mustang. *Her* Mustang.

"Better," he rasped. And then he saw the array of things on the table. He honed in on the scalpel. "You planning on using those on me?"

"Unless I can get you to change your mind about going to the hospital, yes." Maybe if she was lucky, he'd pass out again.

Kane shook his head. The room tilted slightly, then righted itself. "No hospital."

She didn't think so. Though she knew nothing about him, she had a feeling he was as stubborn as hell. But then, most men thought they knew best—even when they usually didn't.

Going over to the liquor cabinet, she found a partially empty bottle of whiskey. Tony had brought it over the other week to celebrate something. At the moment, she couldn't recall what. Crossing back to the sofa, she offered the bottle to him. "This is going to hurt," she said simply.

But Kane declined the drink. As far as he was concerned, he was still on duty, still needed a clear head. Alcohol made people stupid. It had certainly evaporated his uncle's brain.

"Go ahead," he ordered.

Well, he wasn't a coward, she thought. Faced with having a bullet dug out sans anesthetic, most men would have grabbed the whiskey with both hands.

Picking up the scalpel, Marja inserted it into the wound. She kept one eye on her patient as she began to slowly probe the wound, listening for the sound of metal on metal. His face reddened. She looked for something to distract him.

Coming up empty, she finally asked, "Why don't you want me to take you to a hospital?"

Kane took in slow, small breaths, struggling not to tense up. Trying to focus on her question, he gave her an excuse he thought she'd believe.

"I'm between jobs. How easy do you think it'll be—" sweat was oozing down his brow as she probed deeper "—to get one if they look into my background and see that I was shot? I—" he took a deeper breath, as if that could somehow stand between him and the fiery pain "—don't want to have to deal with a lot of suspicious, annoying questions."

She raised her eyes to his for a second, pausing. "Like why were you shot?"

"Yes, like that."

And then she heard it. That slight noise that told her she'd found her quarry. Metal against metal. Very carefully she went deeper, digging beneath the bullet until she managed to draw it out of the hole it had made. The stranger hadn't made a single sound. What the hell was he made of?

She realized she was holding her breath and let it go

as she deposited the bullet onto the cotton swab on the table. "Why were you shot?"

Pain undulated through him like a marauding snake. Kane took in a deep, shaky breath before answering her.

"Unsuccessful mugging," he finally managed to say. "I didn't have anything to mug. Guy got mad. I pushed him and ran. And he shot me. I kept on running. Until you stopped me with your car." It had gone down differently, all except the last part. But for his purpose and her curiosity, he felt it would do. He looked at the bullet on the table. The bullet she'd removed. He raised his eyes to hers. "I'd say we're even."

Chapter 3

His eyes met hers, held her captive, so that she couldn't look away.

Before Marja could respond to his comment, strains of a popular song came out of nowhere, filling the air.

Her cell phone was ringing.

An alert expression instantly came into the stranger's eyes. But he didn't tell her not to answer, or try to stop her when she took the phone out of her pocket and flipped it open.

Marja had a feeling she knew who was calling even before she glanced at the L.E.D. screen to read the number.

Tania. True to her word, it was approximately fifteen minutes since she'd left. Marja placed the phone to her ear.

"This is Marja," she announced. And then she smiled patiently. She glanced toward the other occupant in the room. "Yes, I'm still alive. And yes, he's still here." She paused, listening and then nodded even though Tania wasn't there to see. "Fine, you do that. Bye."

With one finger against the lid, Marja snapped the phone closed again, aware that the stranger had been watching her closely the entire time. His gaze seemed to delve beneath her skin, as if taking inventory of all her veins and capillaries. It made her feel as if she owed him some sort of explanation, even though she knew she didn't.

"She's just checking to see if you killed me yet," she told him, and saw his eyebrows rise with a silent question. Marja realized that she was getting ahead of herself again. There were pieces missing out of her narrative. "My sister," she explained. "Tania. She helped me bring you up here. You were out, so I couldn't really manage—"

"Are you alone here?" he cut in gruffly, stemming the flow of more words.

She didn't answer immediately, torn between lying to him in the interest of possible self-preservation or telling him the truth, which, if he was a homicidal maniac, could prove dangerous.

Marja decided to settle for something in between.

"At the moment, yes. But that's subject to change." Especially if Tania decided to send in the cavalry no matter what she'd said to the contrary. "Besides, you're here, so technically—" she smiled up at him disarmingly "—I'm not alone."

Her answer earned her a scowl.

The stranger sat up and then swung his long legs off the sofa without any warning. Marja had to jump to her feet to avoid getting knocked off.

He glared at her. "Don't you have the sense you were born with?"

She drew herself up, squaring her shoulders with a touch of indignation. It was bad enough that her parents and sisters took turns lecturing her. She didn't need this from a stranger, especially one she was trying to help.

"I believe that the appropriate thing for you to say here is 'Thank you,'" she told him hotly, "not try to ascertain whether or not I'm a candidate for MENSA."

"MENSA?" he echoed with a dismissive snort. "You're more of a candidate for the morgue." He looked at her as if she only had a tenth of her brain functioning. "Don't you know better than to bring a man you don't know anything about into your apartment?"

If she hadn't, he might have bled to death on that side street before anyone found him. Where the hell did he get off, shouting at her? "Only the ones who're bleeding when they faint—sorry, pass out—" she corrected sarcastically "—at my feet."

He continued glaring at her. This was New York City, people who lived here were supposed to be cautious. Murders were currently down but the overall stats on that were still high. Young, attractive women were supposed to know better than to invite trouble into their homes. "I could have been a murderer."

"Are you?" she asked in a deceptively mild voice that hid her jumping nerves. It was in response not to what he was saying, but to the way he was looking at her, almost through her. Making her feel as if she were completely naked and vulnerable.

Maybe, despite her gut feeling, bringing him here *was* a mistake.

He'd killed people, but only in self-defense. By definition, that wasn't a murderer, so his conscience allowed him to answer. "No, I'm not." His eyes narrowed. "But that doesn't change the fact that I could have been and you took a hell of a chance on bringing me into your home." Still sitting on the sofa, he gingerly slipped his shirt back into place, pulling down his T-shirt over the dressing.

This was going to hurt like a son of a bitch by morning, he judged. It didn't exactly feel like a blissful walk in the park now.

Finished, he glanced in her direction. "You said I passed out in the car."

Slowly, she nodded her head. "You did."

Kane still couldn't fathom how someone who seemed to be reasonably intelligent could actually do something so foolhardy. "Then why didn't you just take me to the hospital? If I was unconscious, I sure as hell wasn't in any shape to give you any trouble."

Marja lifted her chin defensively. "Because you asked me not to."

"And that's enough?" he asked incredulously.

Either this woman was very, very good, he thought, or she was just plain stupid. But she didn't look stupid to him. Naive, maybe, but not stupid. And, his eyes slid over her, he had a feeling that if she was very, very good at something, sainthood had little to do with the matter. Even in his present state, Kane wasn't so far gone as to not notice the woman was drop-dead gorgeous.

Marja nodded in response to his question. "I felt responsible for you," she told him. "So, yes, that was enough for me."

"How old are you?" He wanted to know.

She had no idea why he'd want to know, but she wasn't about to blurt out a number like a suspect being interrogated.

"Older than I look," she informed him.

She was a doctor, but she didn't look as if she was even thirty. There was a freshness to her, despite the smart mouth. He would have hated to see something happen to her because of her generosity—or naïveté.

"You want to live, you'd better learn to be more suspicious," he told her matter-of-factly.

"Fine, next time I hit somebody with a bullet wound in his side, I'll call the police."

"You do that." Subtly drawing in a breath, Kane carefully rose to his feet. The floor beneath them shifted. He paused, waiting for his equilibrium to kick in. It proved to be in no hurry to do so.

The feisty doctor was at his side instantly, lending her support and holding on to him in case he was going to fall.

He didn't pull away immediately.

Kane was aware of her small hands pressed against his body, aware of the scent of her hair—something herbal— shampoo. Aware of her presence, which was too damn close to him. He didn't like it weaving into his system.

"I'm okay," he stormed.

Marja lifted her hands away from him, holding them up like a captured robber surrendering to the police to indicate that she was backing off. "Just don't want you passing out again," she told him.

"I won't." It sounded more like a vow to her than a statement. And then he looked at her.

"Marja." He repeated the name he'd heard her say when she'd gotten on her cell phone. "What kind of a name is that?"

She continued watching him, worried that he might pass out again. "A good one."

He laughed shortly. "I meant, what nationality is it?"

"I'm Polish." Since they were exchanging information of a sort, it occurred to her that she didn't even know his name or anything else for that matter. "You?"

"I'm not."

She should have expected nothing less. "Not exactly talkative, are you?"

He took a tentative step, like a sailor getting back his land legs. "The less you say, the less can be held against you."

She took a step with him so that she could remain in front. "Valid enough point," she agreed, "but I'd like to know your name."

She saw suspicion enter his eyes again. Rather than make her uneasy, it just made her wonder all the more about her unorthodox patient.

"Why?"

She shrugged carelessly. "I like knowing the names of people I take bullets out of." He eyed her sharply. "I'm funny that way."

Did he have something to worry about, after all? "So you can report this?"

If she'd wanted to report this, she would have driven him to the hospital. "I thought we'd gotten past that."

Kane paused a moment. She had a point, he thought. And in a few minutes he was going to walk out the door and, most likely, he'd never see her again. He supposed there was no harm in giving her his first name. "Kane."

The moment he shared that small piece of information with her, Marja's eyes lit up. It made her more sensual, he noted. Damn, he'd been so wound up in laying the groundwork for this case, he'd neglected a very basic need. He'd been too long without a woman. The oversight had to be the reason he was reacting to her. Otherwise, he didn't understand where this pull, this attraction, was coming from.

"As in Cain and Abel?" she asked. "Or as in candy?"

"Neither." He saw that the woman was waiting for something more. "If you're asking me how to spell it, it's K-A-N-E."

"Well, K-A-N-E, do you have a last name?"

He was a suspicious person by nature, having learned early on to volunteer nothing because you never knew when something could come back to bite you on the butt. And she was asking too many questions.

"Yes."

Obviously nothing came easy with this man. It really did make her wonder exactly what his story was. And who had wounded him, not physically but emotionally. Because, assuming he wasn't hiding a criminal past, he was far too reticent not to have a reason for his attitude.

"Is it a state secret?" she prodded.

"No." The doctor with the all-intrusive bedside

manner waited for the rest. He blew out a short breath and gave her the rest of it. "It's Dolan." At least, for the time being, he added silently.

Irish. Maybe that was where the green eyes had come from. Marja nodded. "Well, Kane Dolan, it's nice to meet you."

That was a hell of a strange thing to say, considering the way they'd met. With a grille and iron between them. "Why?"

Didn't he accept anything at face value? She decided it had to be tiring, being Kane Dolan. "Is everything a challenge to you?"

"Pretty much," Kane heard himself saying.

He'd meant it as a flippant retort, uttered to make her back off. But in reality, his answer was pretty dead-on. Since the day he'd come home from second grade to find that his heroin-addicted father had shot and killed his cocaine-inebriated mother and then turned the gun on himself, leaving their tiny, dirty kitchen hopelessly splattered with blood, everything about his life had turned into a challenge. He took nothing on faith, expected nothing to be what it seemed. Because it usually wasn't.

Kane came to a stop by the front door. He needed to get going before she had someone show up and start asking awkward questions.

"Thanks for patching me up," he muttered, reaching for the doorknob.

She felt as if she was releasing a wounded bird, not yet fully healed. "When was the last time you ate?" Marja asked suddenly.

He'd just expected her to say goodbye, to be relieved that he was on his way. The question, coming out of nowhere, caught him off guard and he turned to her. Maybe he hadn't heard right.

"What?"

"When was the last time you ate?" Marja repeated, enunciating each word slowly, as if she was talking to someone who was submerged in a tank of water and had trouble hearing.

"Today," was the best he could do. "I don't look at my watch when I eat." He tacked the latter on dismissively. Maybe that was uncalled for, he thought. She seemed to be an irrepressible do-gooder. The woman was in for some major disappointments in her life. He tried to set her straight, at least about the person he was supposed to be. "Look, I'm not homeless and I'm sure as hell not your personal crusade—"

She had her doubts about the first part. He wasn't dirty and his face wasn't leathery and worn from the elements, but that didn't mean that he wasn't down on his luck. There was plenty of that going around these days, she thought.

"You said the mugger had nothing to mug," she reminded him.

So that was it. She thought he had no money, no place to stay. No regular meals. "That's because I left my wallet at home. I find that if you don't carry it, they can't steal it," he told her very simply.

"You've been mugged before," she guessed.

"Yeah." In reality, there was no "before." This was the first time. And it would be the last, he silently promised himself. No one was going to get the drop on him, ever.

Again, Kane reached for the doorknob and this time he actually managed to take hold of it and pull the door open before the doctor said anything else.

"What kind of work are you out of?"

More questions. But it was a small world and you never knew how things ultimately played out or whose path you were going to cross in the near future. So he sighed and faced her and her endless barrage of questions. He knew he could just walk out, but the bottom line was that she had helped him when she was under no obligation to do so. Maybe he owed her a little courtesy—as long as she didn't push it.

Hooking his thumbs in his belt, he gave her a long, penetrating look. "You planning on writing a bio on me, Doc?"

If he thought he could intimidate her—and with that look she was *sure* that was what he was thinking—he'd failed.

"I just thought I might know someone who could give you a job." She was thinking of her father's security company. Kady's husband, Byron, a former bodyguard and ex-cop, worked there along with a number of other people. Not to mention that Kane's demeanor reminded her of Tony, Sasha's husband. Tony was a homicide detective. On the job, they didn't come grimmer than him.

Both men—Tony and Kane, had the same tight-lipped temperament, the same slow, probing nature. Maybe Kane could find a career in some aspect of security work. If she could get him to answer questions without putting up a fight.

"What is it that you do?" she asked.

He moved his shoulders in a vague shrug, stifling a wince as his left side issued a protest. "This and that," he told her.

"Well, that sounds flexible enough." Even if the man didn't, she added silently. He seemed forbidding. And she had a feeling it wasn't just a facade. "I could call—"

He cut her off. The last thing he wanted was for her to find him a job. That was being taken care of even as he stood here with her.

"I said we were even," he insisted. "You don't owe me anything."

It wasn't tit for tat in her book. She believed in free form. "I don't work that way," she told him, noticing a puzzled expression on his face. "With checks and balances. You need a job, I might know of somewhere to place you, that's all I'm saying."

He had to continue being blunt. She wasn't the type to retreat if he took her feelings into account.

"I take care of myself," he informed her in no uncertain terms.

Her eyes lowered to the wound she had just finished stitching and dressing. Maybe he could have done it on his own, but most people don't like to sew their own flesh back into place.

"I'm sure you can."

The tone wasn't exactly sarcastic, but close, he thought. Turning the knob, Kane pulled the door open. Only then did he nod at her.

"See you around, Doc."

He meant it as a parting, throwaway line. Which was a shame, he caught himself thinking. Because in another lifetime, she would be the kind of woman he should have pursued—if he were into the whole hearth-and-family type thing. He could tell, just by looking at her, that she was. Women like that were best left alone. Because he wasn't into that. And nothing good ever followed in his wake.

She was at the door, less than a hair's breadth behind him. "You're going to have to change that dressing tomorrow," she called after him.

He didn't turn around, but he did nod. "I can do it."

"And don't get it wet," Marja added, raising her voice.

"Dry as a bone," he promised, raising his hand over his head to indicate that he'd heard her as he kept on walking.

"And—" She stopped abruptly as her cell phone rang again.

He allowed himself a dry laugh under his breath. "That's probably your sister, checking to see if I've done away with you yet," he guessed.

The next second he'd turned a corner and was out of view.

Turning back into the apartment, she closed the door behind her and glanced at the phone's screen. He was right, it was Tania. Had it been a full fifteen minutes yet? She didn't think so.

She knew that Tania meant well, but there were times when she felt so smothered by her sisters and her parents that she could scream.

"I'm still breathing, Tania," she announced as she opened her cell phone.

"Good," she heard Tania say, "then you won't freak Jesse out when he gets there."

Her back against the door, Marja slid down to the floor, closed her eyes and sighed. "You woke up Jesse."

"No," Tania was quick to correct her, "he was still up. Working on some blueprints for a new building by Lincoln Center." She didn't bother to keep the pride out of her voice. Jesse was an up-and-coming architect and someday people were going to point out his buildings to one another.

"Call him and tell him not to come," she ordered her sister. "Kane's gone."

"Kane?" Tania echoed. "Who's Kane?"

"Mr. Bullet Wound Guy."

Tania didn't bother to stifle her sigh of relief. "Thank God. Now put the chain on."

Marja rose to her feet again. Odd, but she could still feel Kane's presence on the apartment, still all but feel his hand on her wrist when he'd first come to. "I will, now call Jesse off. Let the poor man get some rest."

"Will do."

The line went dead.

Marja's insides didn't.

Chapter 4

Sometimes Kane couldn't help wondering if some master plan existed out in the universe, or if things just happened in a haphazard, random pattern.

By all rights, someone with his background should have been dead by now, or pretty damn well close to it. Both of his parents had succumbed to addiction while still in their early teens and the uncle, his father's brother, Gideon, he'd been sent to live with after their untimely murder-suicide demise, had been long on alcoholism, short on patience. He'd barely survived the beatings.

Social services had stepped in after that, when one of his teachers had reported the frequent bruises he'd tried in vain to hide.

Being passed around from foster home to foster home had been no picnic, either. He'd literally closed up inside. After that, he'd taken to periodically running away. Being on his own was preferable to being under someone else's thumb.

Kane had learned from a very early age how to take care of himself. It came about out of necessity because he'd known that there was no one else around to do it, or to even care if he lived or died. His parents hadn't. His uncle certainly hadn't and neither had any of the families he'd been shipped to like a piece of tattered, hand-me-down clothing. No one had.

He supposed the only reason he hadn't turned to a life of crime was that the thought of being confined in a cage made his chest tighten and the air stop dead in his lungs. Unlike so many who took to that way of life, he knew the odds against him and he was pessimistic enough to believe that no matter how clever he might be, prison would be his ultimate destination.

Permanently tossed out of the system and on his own at eighteen, he'd done the only thing someone with no money and an ability to survive the most adverse conditions could do. He'd joined a branch of the military. Specifically, he'd taken to the air force. It was there that he'd wound up being tapped for Special Forces, which further developed his unique survival abilities.

Somewhere along the line, bit by bit, he'd earned a degree in criminology. So by the time he'd returned to civilian life, joining an organization that could make use of his special skills—one of which was being able to terminate a man's existence using only his thumbs— seemed like a very logical choice.

And that was how he and the CIA came to a meeting of the minds.

Fully grounded, Kane had no illusions about what he did. It wasn't glamorous, but he felt it was damn necessary. And it got his adrenaline pumping, giving him a reason to get up every morning. Not having anyone to worry about or to come home to at the end of the day freed him to do other things.

At times he had to admit, if only to himself, that he wondered what it would be like to have a wife and 2.5 kids. Especially the .5 part. But in truth, all that was utterly foreign to him. He had no reference base, no happy childhood or adolescence to draw on. His had been the kind of childhood that easily bred serial killers.

Or loners.

Which was what he was. A loner.

He supposed he'd always be one, which was all right because he never made any long-term plans. The kind of life he led, working for the Company, did not inspire people to set up IRA accounts for their old age. Few ever attained that status and those who did, usually died of boredom, leaving their funds untouched for the most part.

He liked what he did for a living as much as he could like anything. And making a difference, however minor, mattered to him, again, as much as anything in his life could matter to him.

While he had few rules, there were two he followed. Don't get attached and don't screw up. Simple. And demanding.

Kane supposed he'd been born jaded, which was as good a way as any if you had to be born at all. Being born jaded saved time, because eventually, everyone was stripped of their hopes and illusions. The end result was jadedness. He firmly believed this was inevitable. He'd just gotten a head start.

"Well, everything looks to be in order," the shapely blonde reviewing his forms said. She carefully placed the three sheets on her spotless desk and flashed a broad smile at him.

He wondered what she'd say if she knew the only reason the position he was applying for had opened up was that certain people had persuaded James Dulles, an orderly in excellent standing with the hospital, to take an extended vacation in another part of the country. That was because he needed this position, needed an excuse to be on the hospital premises in a capacity where he could slip in and out without actually being noticed.

No one really noticed orderlies in a hospital unless there was a mess to mop up. Otherwise, they could move around like shadows, having the run of the place. Since they had the grunt work, no one questioned their presence no matter where they were found—other than perhaps the ladies' restroom.

The Company intended to place two or three more of their operatives, men he'd worked with before, at Patience Memorial Hospital. Placing them as the "vacancies" that would suddenly come up in the next couple of days. But he was the center of this. It was his operation to pull off or screw up. So far, his track record was perfect and he intended to keep it that way.

The woman who headed Patience Memorial's Human Resources Department smiled at him. He smiled back. It would be interesting to find out her reaction to the fact that he knew more about Carole Reed than she knew about him. He knew she was divorced, currently between boyfriends and didn't like being unattached. The way she gazed at him told him she was considering him as a possible candidate, someone to dally with as a bridge between the significant others.

Carole looked down at the form. "Says here you worked in two different hospitals in L.A." She raised her eyes to his face. "Tell me, why'd you decide to settle in New York?"

He knew she was a California girl herself. Knew why she'd picked New York. "I like the change of seasons," he told her. "And having everything I could need within walking distance."

Her eyes brightened and she nodded. She came very close to saying, "Me, too." But instead said, "Good enough. Well, your references are impeccable and you sound like you'll be a good addition to our little family." Little was a whimsical term, seeing as how the teaching hospital was one of the larger ones in the city. Carole reached out across her desk, her hand extended. "Welcome to Patience Memorial."

Rising slightly in his seat, Kane took the offered hand and held it a beat longer after he shook it. His smile was warm, charming. Inviting. As befitted the persona he'd assumed.

As always when he was on a job, he was performing. He found that he preferred it that way. When he was someone else, he could do whatever was needed of him without a second thought.

The baggage he carried around only materialized when he was being himself.

"Thank you," he replied heartily, releasing her hand with just a trace of reluctance he knew the woman would appreciate.

Carole tossed her head. Long, straight blond hair floated over her shoulder. "You start tomorrow, bright and early at seven."

It had taken him every shred of time, morning and night, to get everything in place. He was eager to get going. "I could start today," he told her.

The woman laughed lightly, as if he'd told a joke. "Tomorrow will be fine." Taking a square of paper from a green dispenser on her desk, Carole wrote a room number down for him. She handed it to him before she got up from her chair. "Report to this department tomorrow. Raul will show you the ropes. He's a little snippy in the mornings," she warned, "but he doesn't mean anything by it. Try not to get on his bad side—or to take anything he says before noon too personally."

"I try not to get on anyone's bad side," he told her, and for the most part, that was true. Getting on someone's bad side meant getting noticed and his goal had always been the exact opposite, no matter what the situation.

Carole rose slowly, like a model who knew that every set of eyes in the room was trained on her. In this case, there was only one set to look at her, but an audience was an audience.

"That's a very good philosophy," she told him brightly. And then, Carole escorted Patience Memorial's newest employee to the door of her office and once again smiled invitingly just before he left.

He could have had her, he thought, walking away from her office. Probably right then and there on her desk if he'd turned up "Dolan's" charm a notch. The physical coupling would have satisfied the gnawing hunger that the woman who'd bandaged him up had aroused. But again, it would have drawn too much attention his way and he couldn't afford that now. Not if his assignment was to have a successful resolution.

He would have to put up with the damn gnawing.

The details of his assignment were nebulous and sketchy at best. Over the last three weeks, their specialists monitoring the Middle East had picked up international chatter, a lot of it, focusing on a possible terrorist threat occurring at Patience Memorial. The probable target in that case would be the Jordanian ambassador's daughter, Yasmin. The twenty-two-year-old woman was arriving at some unspecified date in the near future to undergo a delicate operation. She had a tumor that had intricately woven itself through her brain.

Two of the country's foremost brain surgeons were going to perform the surgery. One was flying in from the west coast, the other had been on the staff of Patience Memorial for over ten years.

Whether the threat came in the form of a kidnapping—something he highly doubted because of the ambassador's contingent of bodyguards—or a bombing, he didn't know. No one did. That only meant he had to be ready for anything—which also included the very real, frustrating possibility nothing would happen.

The enemy enjoyed playing their little war of nerves, enjoyed planting chatter to unnerve the opposition. They made sure to plant enough rumors so that everyone was in a hypervigilant state. There would be so many false rumors until the real one came and if the public had gotten blasé about the rumors, it would turn a deaf ear to the chatter just when it should be listening closely. Much like the old fable about the boy who cried wolf.

But all that was for the movers and the shakers to sort out and deal with. He was just a foot soldier on the front lines, determined to remain alert to any and all threats. He was there to dismantle the bomb if necessary, to defuse possible volatile situations whenever possible, regardless of the personal consequences.

And that was why he was so good for the job. Because there was no one to take into account when he thought about so-called "personal" consequences. No one would mourn him, no one would cry if he never walked through another doorway.

No one would know that he'd ever existed.

Which was just the way it was supposed to be, he reminded himself.

The thought left Kane cold, even though it was of his own making.

"Kane?"

He was on the first floor, weaving his way through the various connecting corridors, on his way out of the building. The moment he heard his name, he stopped dead.

Someone knew him. But who? There was a quizzical inflection in the woman's voice, as if she was surprised to find him here.

That makes two of us.

The voice was vaguely familiar, but before he could access the mental database he kept in his head, the owner of the melodic voice had reached him and stood before him.

The woman who'd removed his bullet. Marja.

He didn't know if this was good or bad.

"It is you," Marja breathed in surprise.

On a break, she was rushing to the tiny gift shop to see if she could pick up a card that eloquently apologized for forgetting a friend's birthday. Eloquently because she'd missed the date by almost a month, which was bad, even for her.

She'd almost reached the shop's door when her attention had been drawn to the man who'd just walked by the gift shop. The set of the shoulders, the gait, everything whispered of familiarity, teasing her brain like a trivia question she knew the answer to, but was just out of reach.

And then, she knew. It had taken her less than a heartbeat to recognize him.

Only a week ago, she'd removed the bullet and sewn Kane Dolan up. And every day of that week she'd thought about him, usually against her will. Thought about him and wondered if he was all right. If she'd done the right thing, caring for him and not reporting the bullet wound to anyone, not even either one of her brothers-in-law.

Most of all, she wondered if she'd ever see him again.

And now, just like that, here he was, standing right in front of her as if she'd conjured him up out of her imagination. It was almost eerie. Had he come looking for her? Or was he here just to have his wound rebandaged as she'd suggested?

He wasn't saying anything, but his gaze felt intimate, as if all the barriers between a man and a woman had evaporated in the heat of his expression.

She forced herself to say something and not just stand there like a life-size cardboard cutout of herself. "Are you here for a follow-up?"

It *was* her. It wasn't just his imagination. She was talking, although he hadn't heard what she was saying. "What?"

"A follow-up," she repeated. "For your…" Her voice trailed off and then she nodded at his side. "You know."

Yes, he knew. And he'd had that taken care of the day after she'd seen to his wound. His handler had one of the Company doctors examine his wound. The physician had declared his wound well cared for and on the mend. So there was no reason for him to come looking for medical aide.

"No."

Okay, he wasn't here for a follow-up, but he was here. She jumped to the next logical conclusion for his appearance here. He'd come looking for her.

The thought sent a shiver down her spine. She was half wary and, yes, half thrilled. The man before her was a classic "bad boy," the kind every mother worried about and every pubescent girl dreamed about.

"How did you know that I worked at Patience Memorial?"

"I didn't," he said flatly.

Talk about irony. Somewhere in the back of his head Humphrey Bogart's line from *Casablanca*—"Of all the gin joints in all the world, she had to walk into mine"— ran through his brain.

Except that he had been the one to walk into hers. Given his methodical nature, how hadn't he thought to check that out? More importantly, was her being here going to be a problem?

He had no way of telling. For some reason, his usual keen senses and gut feelings weren't coming through.

She should have known better than to think he'd come looking for her. What was the matter with her, anyway? What was she, twelve? No, she was curious. Marja asked, "Well, if you didn't come in for follow-up care, what are you doing here? Visiting someone?"

Kane supposed that he could have just said yes, but that would have led to complications in case their paths crossed again. He couldn't risk being caught in a lie.

So he shook his head and said, "No. I'm here about a job."

"Oh." Well, that was a positive thing, Marja thought. Maybe everything he'd said to her that night was true. That he was temporarily down on his luck. "I could put in a word for you, if you like."

The woman was beaming at him. It was like being caught in a sun storm. Why was she so enthusiastic about his finding a job? He knew he should just tell her that it was already a done deal, that the slinky blonde in HR had hired him, but Marja made him curious.

"Oh?" he asked. "And what kind of word would that be? Doesn't bleed excessively when shot?" he suggested.

He was experiencing amusement, which didn't happen very often in his line of work, or his life for that matter.

She never even blinked. "Something a little less vivid," she promised.

She didn't know why, but the fact that he hadn't made things up as he went along that night, enthused her. Her gut feeling about him hadn't been wrong. Marja was determined to vouch for him.

"Which position?" she pressed. "So that I can get it right."

He stared at her. She was serious. The woman was willing to go to bat for him without really even knowing the first thing about him.

"Why would you do that?" he asked out loud.

"Because you need a job," she answered as if it was the simplest thing in the world. "Because you didn't ransack my apartment when you could have." Her smile widened and he had trouble not being drawn into its aura. "And because you lectured me about letting strange men in."

"And that's why."

"That's why."

Kane shook his head. He supposed her reasoning made sense. Kind of.

"You don't have to bother," he told her. She opened her mouth and he could see that she was getting up a full head of steam to argue with him. He cut her off at the pass. "I already got the job."

He watched, fascinated as her mouth formed a perfect circle.

"Oh. Then congratulations." And then, just when he was certain she couldn't catch him off guard again, the woman with the neat cross-stitch said something that completely surprised him. "Want to celebrate with a cup of coffee? I've got a few minutes before I have to get back, and there's a great little outdoor café halfway down the block."

Few things caught him off guard. He'd been known to handle any dire situation. Several if the occasion called for it. But this was a little thing and little things, personal things, were what startled him.

And he was certainly unprepared for the likes of Dr. Marja Pulaski.

Chapter 5

Just as Kane was about to tell her that he needed to be somewhere else, the loudspeakers crackled to life.

"Paging Dr. Pulaski."

Saved by the disembodied voice, he thought. This way, he didn't have to make up an excuse. There was always the slight chance that it might trip him up later. He'd always found keeping things simple was better.

But when he looked down at the diminutive physician, she appeared to only be partially listening to the page. "Isn't that you?"

Instead of answering, she held up a silencing index finger, waiting. And then it came. "Paging Dr. Sasha Pulaski. You're wanted in Obstetrics."

Marja could only wonder how comforting that had to be to some expectant mother, seeing her sister coming into the delivery room. All eight-and-a-half-months-pregnant of her. These days the staff was taking bets each time Sasha entered the delivery room on whose baby Sasha would wind up delivering first, her patient's baby or her own.

Lowering her finger, Marja smiled at him. "Nope. Not me. They're looking for my big sister." Emphasis on "big" she thought with a fond smile.

"And she's also a doctor?" he asked, just to be sure.

There was no missing the pride in Marja's voice when she answered. "Yes."

Judging from her expression, there was obviously no sibling rivalry between the two, Kane thought. The way there had been between his father and his uncle. Even at six, he'd been made very aware of it. The really odd thing was, once his father was gone, it actually seemed to get worse. He could remember his uncle ranting and raving, his rage growing, about all the times his father had cheated or duped him out of one thing or another. The more that Uncle Gideon drank—and he drank from the moment he walked in at night—the worse it got. And he was always on the receiving end of his uncle's ire.

Kane looked at the woman standing before him. "Here?" he asked.

"Yes." She nodded, grinning. It always seemed to take people by surprise the first time they discovered that there were five of them and that they were all doctors, associated with the same hospital. "We're all here."

All. He took that to indicate that there were more than just two involved. "How many in 'we'?"

Marja paused before finally answering. "Five."

"Five siblings?"

Kane couldn't imagine one family voluntarily having more than a couple of kids, unless, of course, there was money in it, like the third foster family he'd found himself with. The Skylars periodically juggled five, seven foster kids at a time. Ellen Skylar was decent enough, doing what she could to make the experience bearable, but Fred Skylar was in it purely for the money. Money he took for his own, shortchanging the children whose care he was entrusted with, cheating them out of even the most basic of things like food and clothing so that he could have the things he wanted but couldn't afford.

"Five sisters," Marja clarified, sinking her hands deep into the pockets of her white lab coat.

As she did so, she shifted her weight to the balls of her feet, leaning slightly forward. He half expected her to start bouncing. It struck Kane that she seemed to be the embodiment of barely harnessed energy.

"All doctors." It wasn't really a question the way it came out, but he was having trouble with the concept. How did five doctors emerge from one family?

Amused by what she took to be his confusion, Marja nodded. "All doctors."

And they got along well enough and were deemed good enough by the powers-that-be at Patience Memorial, a hospital he'd learned a great deal about in a very short amount of time. Most important of which was that the hospital was considered one of the best all-around hospitals in the country.

"Here," he repeated.

They seemed to be going around in circles. At any

other time, she wouldn't care. But right now, it was eating up her free time.

"Yes, here. Are you sensing a pattern, Kane?" she asked.

"Your parents must be rolling in money to afford to put five of you through medical school."

The cost of things was always his first thought, maybe because when he was growing up, he'd never known more than a dollar or two in his pocket. There was never enough money for anything. His very first memory was hunger, followed closely by fear. He conquered the latter, knowing that not being afraid was his only strength against the adults who were in charge of him. And he learned to ignore the former. It was all part of survival.

The image of her parents rolling in money made her laugh. She only wished it was true. For their sake, not her own.

"Not hardly." Marja glanced down at her watch. The seconds were ticking away. She threaded her arm through his, taking hold of it as if they were old friends rather than strangers. "C'mon, let's go get that coffee and I'll fill you in on the entire saga of the Pulaskis— and then you can tell me yours."

He wasn't looking to find out any more about this talkative woman and he certainly wasn't about to tell her anything about his own family. Nothing had been put in place for him to tell. A family back story hadn't been considered necessary by his handler before he'd gone undercover.

"Mine?"

She tugged on his arm a little because he'd stopped walking. She was leading him to the side exit, which was closer to the coffee shop. "Your saga, your background, your family."

He made a quick decision, shedding layers in his mind. "That'll be real short. There isn't any."

The electronic doors lethargically parted for them.

"No background?" she asked incredulously. "You sprang up, whole, the night I met you? Like Athena out of Zeus' head?"

He had no idea what she was talking about, other than she was referring to some Greek, or maybe it was a Roman, god. Gods didn't interest him. Kane reasoned that he and the gods were even there. He figured he didn't interest them, either.

"No," he said, following her out of the building as she maintained her light but firm grip on his arm. "No family."

Marja stopped walking. When she turned to look at him, he saw instant compassion spring into her eyes. Could she just do that, turn it on and off at will? Were her emotions that close to the surface?

What else was close to the surface?

The question teased him before he banked it down.

"Oh, I'm sorry," Marja told him, her grip turning into a soft, light touch against his arm.

"Don't be." He bit the phrase off.

Clearly sentiment of any kind made him uncomfortable, she thought. Especially when he felt he was the recipient of pity. She could tell by the defensive tone he used.

"That wasn't pity," she told him. "That was sympathy. Or maybe a little fear, too."

"Fear?"

She nodded, resuming her rather vigorous pace. "I couldn't image life without my family. I carp about them," she admitted, "being the youngest and all, but the world would have been a much colder place if I hadn't grown up with four older sisters to look out for me and Josef and Magda Pulaski to fuss over me as they gave me their rules and watched over me."

Kane just shrugged carelessly in response. It was a defensive gesture, she decided.

"And as for my family being rich, I only wish— because that would have made it easier on my parents. They both came from Poland. Escaped from Poland would be a better word for it," she corrected. "It was still under the U.S.S.R.'s thumb when they managed to smuggle themselves out. They were determined that their children would grow up to be anything they wanted to be—because they would grow up free." It was, she knew, her father's favorite word. Free. "My dad eventually got on the police force. In between having babies, Mama took any job that would have her so that we could have a better life than she and my father'd had." To bring her point home, she added with affectionate pride, "Mama cleaned offices in Rockefeller Center for a while."

"And you all became doctors." It was still rather hard to fathom.

"We all became doctors," she confirmed. And each of them had gone into a different field of medicine.

"How?" he asked. The price of a regular college education was high these days. Medical school was all but prohibitive. Multiplying that times five bordered on fantasy.

"Loans, hard work," she enumerated. "My dad held down a couple of jobs more than once. My mother did what she could. Cleaning, cooking for other people." It was the latter that had finally taken off. Thanks to her father's constant encouragement, Mama was set to open up her own restaurant. They were almost as excited about that as they were about Sasha's baby. Almost. "And the second each of my older sisters would graduate, she'd work to repay her own loans and to donate money to the next sister in line."

Coming to a crosswalk, he glanced to see if there was any traffic. Marja had made the survey for him and now dragged him across the street.

He shook his head. "Hell of a program."

He'd get no argument from her, she thought. "Yes, it is. But more important than that, there's nothing like knowing that there are people who have your back, no matter what."

Growing up, she'd been resentful at times when her family stuck its collective nose into her business. But she'd come to realize that they had all done it out of love. Resentment turned into appreciation.

Not that she intended to say anything out loud just yet. She did want a measure of privacy. And her sisters shouldn't think they'd won the war. As for her parents, well, she figured that after four other daughters, all headstrong in their own fashion, her parents knew that she loved and appreciated them, even if she had sometimes acted otherwise.

Still holding on to his arm, Marja brought Kane into a small, fairly occupied coffee shop. There were five people ahead of them, all from the hospital, all dressed in scrubs of some sort, blue for medical staff, green for housekeeping.

A quick glance around the area told her that they were the only two there, other than the people behind the counter, in civilian clothes—if she didn't count her lab coat.

"You were an orphan?" she asked him without any preamble.

He didn't like talking about his past, didn't like even thinking about it. Kane stared at the back of the man's head in front of him. "Pretty much."

Marja rolled his answer over in her head. It was far from definitive. Did that mean he had a parent or parents who gave him up because they couldn't—or wouldn't—provide for him? Or did he mean that he'd lost his parents at an older age and didn't really consider himself an orphan? The temptation to ask him outright was very strong—she'd always been one who wanted to know things, *everything* about any given situation or person.

As far back as she could remember, she'd hated secrets, hated being kept in the dark. But in this case, asking when he chose not to elaborate would have been tantamount to being insensitive. And she had a feeling that if she pressed, he'd tell her nothing at all. Or worse, make things up.

So instead she nodded, a look of genuine compassion for what she imagined he'd gone through entering her eyes. "I'm sorry."

Compassion, pity, it didn't matter. He didn't want it. Needing either made a man weak or vulnerable, and he could afford neither. "Don't be," he told her crisply. "I survived."

"That which doesn't kill you makes you stronger?" she guessed. He seemed like the type who'd advocate a mantra like that.

He moved his shoulders in a vague shrug. "Something like that." They were next in line. He glanced at her and nodded toward the counter as he raised his voice to be heard above the whirr of two machines busy mixing special orders. "What would you like?"

The answer that rose to her lips was automatic. "To make you smile."

Her reply—and the look in her eyes—took him aback. That was twice she'd caught him off guard, he thought, and that didn't even take into account the fact that he hadn't expected to run into her here.

"Make him smile later. He's talking about your order," the tall man behind the counter said. It was obvious that he was extremely harried.

Because she frequented the shop religiously, she was accustomed to the server's less than friendly manner. For her part, she flashed him a smile. "Sorry. Mocha cappuccino."

The server shifted small brown eyes in Kane's direction. "You?"

Kane had never been one to follow fads. He kept up on things only insofar as they affected his work. For the most part, he liked the basics and saw no reason to change. "Coffee. Black."

The server, Sylvester, according to his name tag, waited. When nothing further followed, Sylvester looked disdainfully at him. "That's it?"

"That's it," Kane replied in a monotone.

The disdain increased, backed up with a sneer. "Don't they have vending machines where you are?"

Millie, the woman who owned this particular franchise, was over at the far end of the counter, arranging the latest batch of biscotti cookies she'd just taken from the oven. Ears like a bat, she honed in on the conversation.

"Sylvester, stop harassing the customers," she ordered. Millie was a heavy-set, jovial-looking woman with a beatific smile that she now flashed as she came forward. "Ignore my son," she told Kane. "He's a coffee snob." Her smile widened, displaying a set of perfectly matched, brilliantly white dentures. "Customer's always right," she added, parroting a century's old sentiment that was, for better or worse, carved into the hearts of business owners throughout the country.

Moving her son aside, she took over filling the order. Done, she placed the two large containers on the counter. "That'll be twelve-fifty," she informed Kane cheerfully.

Out of the corner of her eye, Marja saw Kane take out his wallet as she reached for her own. She had hers out faster.

"I invited you," she reminded him. "That makes it my treat."

Kane always tried to stay out of people's debts, no matter how minor. He didn't like feeling as if he owed anyone anything. Besides, he was of the old school. Men didn't allow women to pay for them.

"I can pay for coffee," he growled. "Even if it is overpriced."

Though Millie continued to smile, her teeth were slightly clenched as she said, "The nearest diner is—"

Marja was quick to cut in, forestalling a possible flare-up. "That's all right," she told the woman, placing a twenty on the counter. "We don't need to know that. Keep the change."

The twenty was gone in a flash, disappearing into the register and coming to rest in a special slot. The drawer rang melodically as it was closed again. "Thank you. Come again."

Picking up his container, he followed Marja back outside. "You always throw your money around like that?"

"Only when the person I'm with insults the server." She looked around for a table for them. "Good thing you're not a doctor," she told him. "You'd really have to work on your bedside manner."

Spotting an empty table, he took the lead. "My bed-side manner's fine, thanks," he told her, sitting. "I just don't like seeing people being taken advantage of."

She slid into the chair opposite him, tucking her legs to the side. "What people?"

Prying off the lid, he took a tentative sip of his coffee. "Anyone who pays that ridiculous price for a container of coffee." And then he narrowed the playing field, looking at her. "You."

The answer made her smile. "So, you're a frustrated knight in shining armor. I'll keep that in mind." Following his lead, she took the lid off her container and then raised it in a toast. "To your new job. By the way—"

she sipped slowly, careful not to burn her tongue "—what is it?"

"I'm an orderly." He watched her face for any sign of disdain, waited for it actually, and almost felt a tinge of disappointment when it didn't materialize. He decided to push the envelope a bit. "Sure you want to be seen fraternizing with me?"

Had she missed something here? "Why wouldn't I?" Marja asked.

He'd seen people pull rank for far less reasons. "You're a doctor."

She nodded, not sure what that had to do with it. "That's what the diploma in my office says."

He continued watching her expression as he pointed out the obvious. "And I'm a glorified janitor."

Is that how he thought of himself? Or was he saying that just to see her reaction? There was nothing simple about this man.

"No, you're not," she told him, "but even if you were—so?"

"So in the scheme of things at the hospital, I'm beneath you."

"Not yet." Her eyes widened in horror as the sound of her own voice sank in. "Oh God, did I just say that out loud?" The surprised look that melted into a smile on his lips told her that she had. Marja could feel her face reddening. "I did, didn't I?" She did her best to sweep the comment under the rug. "Sorry about that, just a play on words." She hid behind her coffee for a second, sipping very slowly as she regrouped. "I don't know what kind of a caste system you think we have going on here at P.M.," she said, placing the container back on the table, "but you're wrong. There is *no* caste system," she told him firmly. "Everybody puts their scrubs on one leg at a time around here."

He took a deep breath as the image of her doing just that, of putting on her scrubs, or rather, of taking them off, one leg at a time, flickered through his head. Kane allowed himself a moment to savor the image as it drifted through his brain.

The corners of his mouth curved ever so slightly as he did.

Chapter 6

"Nothing?"

"Nothing."

Kane frowned as he looked down into his coffee cup, the overhead light shimmering across the inky surface. Across from him in the corner booth was Frank Rosetti. Frank was his handler, the man who acted as his conduit, getting him information from the Company. In this case, information that enabled him to block any terrorist attack at the well-known hospital.

Except that right now, Frank was not providing any information. The forty-something man with the fifty-something face maintained that there was nothing further to report.

Frank nodded his head, the same light that was caressing the surface of Kane's coffee was cruelly highlighting the fact that Frank Rosetti had no real need of a comb.

"The chatter stopped," Kane said incredulously, having trouble wrapping his head around what Frank had just told him.

"The chatter stopped," his handler confirmed.

Kane regarded the man for a long, silent moment. He'd worked with Frank ever since he'd signed on with the Company, although they never socialized outside the job. Not that Frank hadn't tried once or twice. But they worked well enough together, which was all Kane figured was required.

Right now, he could feel frustration setting in. This didn't make sense. "If I wanted to hear my words fed back to me, Frank, I'd be having this conversation with my mirror, not you."

Shoulders that were just a little too small for the rest of the man's five-ten frame rose and fell. "What do you want me to say, make something up? There's nothing." Leaning forward, Frank lowered his voice to almost a whisper. "Everything and anything that had to do with the ambassador's daughter's pending surgery and the hospital has just stopped. Dried up. Nada. Zip. Nothing," he repeated.

Kane's frown cut right down to the bone. "That just doesn't sound right."

"No, it doesn't," Frank agreed with a sigh, scratching his bald pate.

Kane leaned back in his seat, stretching his long legs out before him until the tip of his shoe touched the bottom of the opposite seat. Was the Company pulling the plug on this operation? He didn't think that was a wise idea, but for now, he kept that to himself.

"So," he began, studying Frank's face, "what do you want me to do?"

Experience had shown that when there was smoke, there was fire. Which would likely amount to a loss of lives. The price was too steep for them to just walk away.

"Stick around anyway. Just in case." It was a judgment call, Kane decided. Frank's butt would be on the line if he was wrong. "There was too much talk before for there to be nothing now."

Kane nodded slowly. After finishing the now cold coffee, he put the cup down. "They could just be messing with our minds. Or trying to throw us off." It wouldn't be the first time, either. "There might be a different target altogether and this little shadow-boxing episode was just a diversion."

Word had it that before joining the Company, Frank had been an accountant. Kane sensed the man sometimes missed the security of straightforward answers.

Frank blew out a long, shaky breath. "Yeah, the Company's thought of that. But you're in, might as well stay in until the ambassador's kid is back on a plane, bound for home."

Kane only knew the names of three other operatives involved in this. There were more in play, of that he was certain, their identities known only to Frank and the powers-that-be. It took the issue of betrayal off the table. "And Montgomery, Cannova and Sanchez?" Cannova had been installed as a security guard more than a month ago; Sanchez worked in the cafeteria where, with his gregarious personality, he struck up conversations at random, seeking tidbits of information. As for Montgomery, he was an orderly, like him.

Frank nodded. "They're staying, too."

Maybe all this *was* for nothing, Kane thought, and they were overreacting. "The ambassador's going to have a hell of a lot of security in place on his own. They say he's paranoid."

Frank laughed shortly. "Aren't we all? Just because you're paranoid doesn't mean they're not out to get you." He paused. "You making nice with everyone?" he asked flippantly. Kane said nothing, merely looked at him. "Yeah, right, what am I thinking, this is you. Just continue doing what you're doing. Nose around without drawing any attention to yourself."

"I'm not a rookie, Frank."

"Not even on your first day," Frank agreed.

His first day on the job, Kane recalled, had been September 11, 2001. A baptism by fire. Hell of a way to start.

Frank's sarcastic question, whether he was "making nice," made him think of Marja. Lots of things made him think of her. He'd been at the hospital for all of one week and in that time, he'd managed to catch a glimpse of her every day, sometimes without her knowing. To what end, he couldn't say, other than she was easier on his eyes than she was on his brain. She seemed to be embedding herself there and he didn't like it.

He forced himself to think about the Jordanian ambassador's daughter again. Right now, his general assignment had him on the first floor, where the operating rooms were located. He wanted to be in the general vicinity when the ambassador's daughter was wheeled in—and out again. But he also was going to need a reason to be in the tower suites. He'd managed to get a look at the preregistration logs when one of the clerks had stepped away. A little quick finger work on the keyboard had him learning that the ambassador had retained the largest suite in the hospital's tower for his daughter—although no actual date had been entered, just the month.

The thinking, Kane assumed, was that they needed the extra space for her bodyguard detail. He had yet to discover if the suites on either side would be occupied, and if so, by whom. But he was working on it. In general, the hospital tower suites were reserved for VIPs and the family members of VIPs. The price tag on one of them was high. But not all terrorists were poor.

And not all terrorists looked alike. They didn't come neatly labeled, either. It was his firm belief that to pull anything off, inside people were going to be required. He needed to ascertain who before it was too late. Which was where being assigned to the E.R. came in handy. Hospital staffers talked to relieve the tension. And he listened.

He hadn't made up his mind whether Marja putting in hours in the E.R. was a plus or a minus. The one thing he did know was that she distracted him.

Kane glanced at his watch and abruptly straightened his torso. "Anything else you want to share with me?" he asked Frank. "My break's almost over."

The handler looked a little surprised, then smiled.

He picked up the baseball cap from the seat beside him and put it on. "Nice to see you following rules for a change."

"I always follow rules," Kane told him, rising. "They just don't happen to always be yours."

"Don't I know it." Frank sighed. Sliding out of the seat, he looked at Kane. "I figure, since you're collecting two paychecks these days, you'll pick this up." He nodded toward the coffees.

Kane said nothing as he took out a five and two singles from his pocket, leaving them on the table. He left before Frank.

The second he entered the hospital's side doors, the ones that admitted paramedics and their passengers directly into the E.R., Kane found himself engulfed in pandemonium. People ran in one direction or another.

Instantly alert, he focused, scanning the immediate area, anticipating the worst.

But there was no need to remove the small handgun that he kept strapped to his left ankle beneath the green scrubs. A couple of tersely worded questions told him that the commotion seemed to be revolving around the passengers three separate ambulances had brought in. All were victims of a rival gang shoot-out that had spilled out onto a different turf.

"I'm gonna die, I'm gonna die!" the person on the gurney closest to him was screaming. The gang member, soaked in blood, grabbed at a nurse. "I want a priest. Get me a damn priest," he demanded. "I gotta make it right."

Before Kane could do anything to disengage the nurse from the wounded gang member's grasp, Marja came on the scene. Separating the frightened-looking young nurse from the gang member, she took her place beside the gurney and hurried with it to the first available trauma room.

"You're going to be fine," she assured the hysterical gang member.

"I'm holding you to that," he cried, for a moment sounding more like a lost child than the owner of a long rap sheet.

"Show some respect," Kane warned the youth, his voice low but lethal.

Marja looked at Kane in surprise, as if she hadn't already noticed that he was there.

"Not to worry, he will," she assured Kane with a quick flash of a smile, then added, "C'mon, I'm going to need those muscular arms of yours."

She summoned a nurse, an intern and another orderly to come into the small room with them. The others all arranged themselves either on one side of the gurney or the examination table they needed to pull the extremely vocal patient onto.

Kane moved beside her.

"On my count," Marja announced. "One, two, *three!*" Six pairs of hands lifted the corners of the sheet the wounded gang member was on, transferring him onto the examination table.

The second they began moving him, a barrage of expletives exploded from his mouth. Kane lowered his side of the makeshift transport little faster than the others did, jarring the gang member as he came down on the flat surface.

"Hey!" he cried angrily.

Kane gave him a steely, unreadable look. "Sorry, my bad."

Marja slanted a glance in Kane's direction as she reached for a needle to numb the area she needed to probe. "You don't look very sorry," she commented, barely moving her lips.

The expression in his eyes told her he heard. As a doctor, she was honor-bound to treat anyone who needed her. As a person, she could understand Kane's reaction to the gang member and his vicious mouth.

The doors to the trauma room burst open. Two patrolmen made their way in, decreasing an already small space. Harried and very obviously seasoned in the ranks, they gave the impression that they weren't about to go anywhere anytime soon, nor were they about to mollycoddle the wounded gang member.

"We need to ask him some questions," the taller, older of the two said, addressing the statement to the intern rather than Marja.

He attempted to elbow her to the side as he tried to get in closer to the examination table and the patient. It was clear that he would have rather seen the man behind bars than in a hospital.

The patient responded with yet another hail of less than friendly words, some of which had to do with the officer's parentage.

Marja had every respect in the world for law-enforcement officers. As a kid, she'd hung around her father's precinct and two of her brothers-in-law had taken the vow to serve and protect. Still, this was her territory and she intended to call the shots.

"After I'm done, gentlemen," Marja told them firmly, coating her words with a smile.

The gray-haired policeman refused to back off. "Sorry, we have to ask now, little lady. There might not be a later."

"Then I *am* gonna die!" the wounded man sobbed angrily.

"Someday," Marja agreed, raising her voice above the din. "But not today." She looked from one officer to the other. "Please, wait outside," she requested again.

The shorter, heavier set of the two intervened. "Look, Doc—" his small brown eyes swept over her frame "—we've got a job to do—"

"And so does she." Marja wasn't sure how he did it, but Kane had managed to put himself between her and the two policemen, like a human shield. "You let her do hers and then she'll let you do yours." He looked over his shoulder, nodding at the less-than-cooperative patient. "He's not going anywhere," he added with finality. "I give you my word." With that, he began to slowly usher the two away from the exam table.

The patrolmen exchanged glances, looking far from happy about the situation.

"C'mon, Eddie," the heavy-set policeman urged his taller partner, "maybe we can catch a break with one of the other two lowlifes. It's not like there's a shortage of people to talk to."

"Good idea," Kane agreed. He had the two at the doors and he pushed one open.

Eddie quite clearly didn't care for his attitude. "Watch it, pal," he warned. Holding up his hand, he created a tiny space between his thumb and forefinger. "You're this close to being written up for impeding an investigation."

"Just doing my job, guys, trying to let the doc do hers," Kane replied innocently. He didn't, however, budge from where he was standing, which in turn blocked the policemen's access to the suspect.

Eddie bit off an oath under his breath and left with his partner. As the doors closed behind them, Kane turned to Marja. The patient was growing progressively less cooperative, thrashing around like a newly captured salmon on the deck of a fishing boat. "Need anything else?"

"Another set of hands to hold him down would be nice," she responded, raising her voice above the wounded man's ripe curses.

"You don't come near me with that," the man shrieked when he saw the needle. He did his best to bolt off the table.

She stood back, needle raised. The last thing she needed was to have it break off in his arm. "It'll numb the area," she promised.

But the wounded gang member had other ideas. Again he tried to get off the table. "You're not putting nothin' into me. How do I know what that garbage is?" he demanded. The next moment he'd knocked out the orderly closest to him and shoved one of the nurses into the intern. They went down like bowling pins.

Kane reached him, grabbing the side of the man's neck.

The next moment the wounded man slumped back on the table, out cold.

Marja meanwhile had grabbed a sedative, thinking to knock the patient out in her own way. Her eyes went from the patient to Kane in open wonder. She didn't quite understand what had just happened here. "Who are you, Mr. Spock?"

"Just a little something I picked up in the air force," he lied. It wasn't the air force that had taught him how to render a man unconscious by using pressure applied to just the right neurological spot, it had been the Company. "I didn't take you for a Star Trek geek," he said, amused.

"My dad used to watch the reruns. I watched with him. Quality time," she added.

Kane had turned to help the nurse back to her feet as the intern scrambled to his. The other orderly was massaging a sore jaw. "Whatever floats your boat," he told her.

Marja took the opportunity to inject the sedative into the gang member's arm, sinking the needle into the mouth of the red devil he had tattooed there. That would keep him out for a while, she thought, putting the needle on the tray. And then she took a closer look at the man's neck. There was an angry red line where Kane had applied pressure.

"Seriously, how did you do that?" she pressed.

"I'll give you a demonstration sometime," he promised. He had no intentions of following up on that.

There was a great deal more to this "orderly" than met the eye, she thought. Marja quickly glanced around at the other occupants in the room. "Let's just keep what happened here to ourselves, all right?"

The nurses and the orderly nodded, a chorus of

"sure" and "fine with me" meeting her request. But the intern frowned, confused. "Aren't we supposed to write up reports about everything that happens during our shift?"

"Yes, but there's no reason why you can't write down the *Reader's Digest* version." She winked at the intern who looked flustered. "All right, let's hurry and get this bullet out before Neanderthal Man comes up for air and round two."

"Benson was right, you know." Marja addressed the words to Kane as they walked out of the trauma room twenty minutes later. The patient, properly handcuffed to the railing, had been taken, still unconscious, to X-ray to make sure that there weren't any internal injuries that were being overlooked.

He stopped by the vending machine and counted out the right amount of change to secure a pack of gum. He'd given up smoking five months ago. The craving, however, had not given him up. So he chewed and pretended that satisfied his craving.

The coins jingled melodically as they made their way into the bowels of the machine. He punched the code numbers marked above the pack of gum. "Who's Benson?"

"The intern." The yellow pack fell with a soft thud. He pushed the glass back and claimed his prize. "Hospital orderlies aren't supposed to act independent of instructions like that."

"Better than punching him out," Kane told her. "That was my first thought." Pulling the wrap off the gum, he offered her one. She shook her head. Kane pulled out a stick, shoving the rest into his pocket. "Besides, he didn't look like someone who would exactly listen to reason. That kind doesn't understand anything but force."

She studied his face. Who *are* you? she wondered not for the first time. "You sound as if you're speaking from experience."

"I've spent my time on the streets," he allowed.

Marja shifted to the other side of the vending machine. It was a tiny alcove that gave them a minimum of privacy. "Tell me about it."

His eyes met hers. "I just did."

"The long version," she prodded.

He shrugged. "Maybe some other time." It was a throwaway line because there wasn't going to be "some other time." His life, past and present, was a private matter, something he wasn't about to share with anyone. He started walking away.

Marja fell into step beside him. "The same time you'll show me that maneuver you performed on the patient?"

"Yeah, the same time as that," he agreed.

"No, you won't," she said with such finality it told him that in some small way, she was on to him.

Kane stopped walking. There was a supply closet at his back. His eyes swept over the rest of the floor. No one was looking their way. Grabbing her hand, he opened the door and then pulled her inside with him.

The breath rushed out of her lungs as tension raced in, accelerating her pulse. Adrenaline flowed through her. She didn't say a word.

"Why do you want to know?" he asked.

She chose her words carefully. "Because sometimes talking about things that bother you helps."

"What makes you think it bothers me?"

"You won't talk about it," she answered simply.

He could feel her breath on his face as she answered. Could feel his gut tightening in anticipation of something he wasn't supposed to be anticipating. "That's kind of a catch-22, isn't it?"

Her eyes were smiling at him. Stirring him. She nodded. "Uh-huh."

He shook his head. "I can't quite figure you out, Doc."

She tried to spread her hands and managed to brush them against his chest. She dropped them to her sides again. "Not much of a puzzle there," she told him. "I'm an open book."

Not from where he was standing, he thought.

And then, despite the logical way he normally conducted his life, despite the ultimate urgency of the situation he'd been sent in to handle, there was nothing else on his mind except for one thing.

Finding out what her lips tasted like.

He'd always been a man to meet a problem head-on.

Chapter 7

She'd known the second Kane had pulled her into the closet that this wouldn't be just some sudden consultation. Nor was it a desperate attempt to secure a measure of privacy for the sole purpose of the exchange of words. And they certainly weren't going to take impromptu inventory, either. At least, not of the supply closet.

So when Kane stopped talking and suddenly framed her face with his hands a pulsating, quick second before he brought his lips down to hers, Marja wasn't surprised. She had been holding her breath until his mouth finally made contact with hers. Which was fortunate because he immediately stole every molecule of air away.

Her air, her thoughts, her very being.

Marja was far from a novice at this. There were a number of relationships, some even semiserious, in her past. But she couldn't recall a single one of those men shaking her down to the very tips of her toes, or making her pulse hammer like the middle passage of *The Anvil Chorus*.

The velvety-soft dimness within the supply closet swiftly tiptoed into total darkness, allowing her to slip into a netherworld where there were no borders. No walls, no ceilings, just space.

Just him.

She could feel her body heating as it moved into his, seemingly on its own power, guided by the gentle yet urgent pressure of his hand against the bottom of her spine.

He was pulling her closer to him.

Or had she fallen into him?

She didn't know, she couldn't tell. She just desperately wanted for this to go on as long as humanly possible.

Forever.

She wrapped herself around him, intensifying the kiss. Giving as well as getting.

This was a mistake.

He tried not to make mistakes, carefully avoiding them because mistakes cost him. Always cost him, one way or another. And yet, knowing this, he still couldn't make himself pull back.

Couldn't break contact.

Couldn't do anything except deepen the kiss and seek out more. Holding her against him like this acutely reminded him just how long he'd been about the business of a covert operative and nothing more.

He wanted more.

He wanted her.

To such a degree that it alarmed him. He'd never, ever been one to lead with anything but cold, hard logic and cold, hard logic dictated that there was no place for this on his immediate agenda.

That didn't seem to matter right now. Not with every inch of his body feeling as if it was on fire.

His mouth still sealed to hers, Kane ran his hands slowly up along the sides of her body. Felt her small, eager breasts as she pressed them hard against his chest. An urgency filled him that was almost impossible to subdue.

More than anything, he wanted to take her. Right here, right now. Take her to rid himself of this damn feeling, this damn itch that was growing to almost unmanageable proportions.

But he couldn't, *wouldn't,* let himself give in to the demands of his body. Because he wasn't a rutting pig. But most of all, because she deserved better.

So, with more willpower than this sort of a situation had ever required before, Kane forced himself to put his hands on her shoulders and pry the two of them apart. Still holding her shoulders, his breath feeling like this hard, physical entity in his throat, he tried not to sound as if he'd just come up for air after diving down too deep.

But he had.

It was damn difficult getting his breath regulated enough to venture a word.

Kane could just about make out her lips in the dim closet. They were curved.

"What?" he asked, needing to know what prompted the smile.

Marja took in a long breath before answering. The man had to know that as a kisser, he probably had no equal. Not on this planet. She wasn't telling him anything he wasn't already aware of.

Still, she forced herself to refrain from running her tongue along her lips, even though she wanted to taste him. "You certainly do go to great lengths to keep from talking."

She was referring to his avoiding her probing questions just before he'd pulled her into the closet, he thought. He played along. "Did it work?"

Marja slowly moved her head from side to side, her smile never wavering. "No, all it did was bring up a whole host of other questions."

Like when they were going to make love, because she knew that was going to happen. Soon. She could feel it in her bones—the ones that hadn't melted down to the consistency of butter.

"Then I'd better get out of here before you start asking them," he said.

And before I start ripping off your clothes, he added silently.

Right now, he had little control over himself and he couldn't allow anything more to happen. Things had a way of snowballing and he was not about to be buried beneath an avalanche, even if she was packed in snow beside him.

His hand on the doorknob, Kane paused and then looked at her over his shoulder. "Why don't I let you go out first?" he suggested. "You don't want people to see us in here together."

Was he bothered by gossip? Or was there some other

reason for secrecy? As for herself, she'd never really cared what people had to say. If they were going to talk about her, they'd talk. Gossip was part of the workplace. For the most part, however, she got along with the people on staff at the hospital. In a way, because her sisters worked here, it almost felt like a second home to her.

But she liked the fact that he was sensitive to gossip on her account. Apparently, the man with the hard exterior had a soft center.

Not to mention he was one incredible kisser.

Amused, touched, she smiled at him and lightly ran her fingers along his cheek. "No, we wouldn't want your reputation to suffer."

Then, with a wink, she was gone.

Damn woman, he thought, uncomfortable with the way she'd shaken things up.

Kane remained in the closet, giving himself to the slow count of twenty. As he mentally ticked off the numbers, he struggled to get his body, and his head, under control again. It wasn't as easy as it should have been.

He couldn't afford to let anything personal get in the way of his assignment. A lot more was riding on that than any sort of trivial physical gratification achieved on his part.

He justified hanging around Marja by telling himself he was trying to build as many contacts throughout the hospital as possible. Justification. He was pretty certain that if there was danger tied into the ambassador's daughter's arrival, someone with Marja's background wouldn't have a hand in it. For one thing, the woman was too involved with her family and with the community.

He'd done his homework on her, again under the guise of gathering information and not because of the crackling electricity between them. He'd discovered that her parents were as patriotic as they came, that she and some of her sisters volunteered at a free clinic whenever possible, caring for people who couldn't afford to pay for medical insurance. There wasn't a hostile, resentful bone in the woman's supple, tempting body. Terrorists were made of different stuff than this.

In addition, she didn't strike him as someone who could be talked into blindly following orders. Terrorists were malcontented masterminds and sheep. She fell into neither category.

…Twenty, he silently declared. Kane reached for the doorknob, only to have it suddenly moved out of his hand. Someone on the other side was opening the door. His brain scrambled for a plausible excuse as to what he was doing here.

Grabbing the closest thing to him—a blanket—he was about to say that the door had closed on him as he'd gone to get a blanket for one of the patients.

He needn't have bothered coming up with the excuse.

Marja was on the other side of the door. "Would you like to grab some pizza tonight?" she asked him, acting as if it were perfectly normal to carry on a conversation with someone standing in the supply closet.

His eyebrows drew together in slight confusion. "You asking me out?"

She backed up so that he could exit the closet. Kane tucked the blanket back into its place. "No, I'm asking you in, actually. My place," she specified. "I believe you already know where it is. Or do you need directions?" she deadpanned.

"No directions," he confirmed. And then he paused. He couldn't let this go any further, no matter how much he wanted it to. "Actually," he told her, "I'm busy tonight."

"Oh." The single word dripped with surprise mingled with disappointment. And then her smile brightened again. "Well, if you change your mind—or stop being busy," she added, tongue in cheek because she just *knew* it was an excuse, "the offer still holds."

And with that, she hurried off to put out the next fire, deal with the next crisis—trying very hard not to dwell on the fact that ten minutes after he had stopped kissing her, her body was still tingling, still wanting to leap to the next level with this man who had come into her life like a huge Christmas surprise.

"Sure you don't want to come with us?" Tania asked for the third time as she stepped into the shoes she'd selected after more than a ten-minute debate.

Marja leaned against the doorjamb leading into her sister's bedroom. She scanned the area, thinking that she'd seen tornado sites on the news that looked more orderly than Tania's room. In response to Tania's question, she shook her head.

"Yes, I'm sure. I have a date with a pizza," she said glibly. Marja glanced at her wristwatch. "The delivery boy should be here any minute."

"Dinner at Le Crepe would be a whole lot better," Tania murmured, distracted.

Tania fumbled with her left earring, trying for the

second time to get the backing mounted onto the minuscule gold post. Succeeding finally, she surveyed the results in her mirror. The earrings hung down to just above her shoulders. She moved her head to watch them swing.

"Agreed," Marja said cheerfully. "But I don't think that Jesse will be overly thrilled to have his sister-in-law-to-be tagging along. He probably has a romantic evening in mind. That usually means two, not three, for dinner."

Tania's eyes met hers in the mirror as she checked her makeup over one last time. "Jesse likes you, Marysia. He likes the whole family," Tania reminded her. "I couldn't marry Jesse, much as I love him, if he didn't get along with all of you," she pointed out.

Marja knew that. Knew that all four of the men her sisters had chosen had miraculously fit neatly into the family structure, even if it hadn't seemed like it at first. Tony, Sasha's husband, had been pretty much of a loner. But they'd all taken him in hand and now he was one of the family as much as any of them. Marja couldn't have been happier for her sisters—and her parents since she knew how much it meant to them to have this kind of harmony.

But it also made her realize that good romantic matches were exceedingly rare. And, most likely, she didn't have one in her future. The men she seemed to gravitate toward were rebels, outsiders. Men who had no talent at fitting in nor the desire to learn. The problem, she knew, was her, not them, because the few down-to-earth, decent-to-the-bone men she'd gone out with had bored her to tears. Her blood hadn't rushed when one of them had kissed her, it had simply sighed—and not in a good way.

Not like with Kane.

Marriage and kids were definitely not in her future, she decided as she watched Tania reapply her lipstick. The thought made her feel oddly sad, which surprised her because, until this very moment, she hadn't realized that she actually wanted that. To have someone other than one of her sisters to come home to. To have children with that someone.

But she still didn't want to settle. Better to give up the dream than to live a life of quiet desperation. She was getting maudlin, Marja silently upbraided herself. Rousing, she forced a smile to her lips as Tania turned away from the bureau.

"You just have yourself a good time." Marja followed Tania to the living room. "Are you two coming back here?" she asked.

Checking through her purse, Tania looked up at her. "Why?"

She just wanted to know if she had the apartment to herself, but saying so would probably make Tania think she had someone coming over and the questions would start. So she made something up.

"I just want to know so I can be presentable instead of sitting around in my cutoffs." She indicated the faded, tattered pair she wore.

Tania grinned and patted her face. "If we come back, little sister, it'll be way past your bedtime." Her eyes shone as she added, "I'm not on call tomorrow."

Good, it was about time Tania took a day off. At

times it seemed like all they did was work. "Planning on dancing until dawn, huh?"

"Or something like that," Tania told her, punctuating her statement with a wink.

Now that didn't make any sense. "And you were inviting me along?"

Slim shoulders beneath the tailored white sheath rose and fell. "Well, since you're not coming, plans can be changed."

She would have been lying if she said she wasn't just the tiniest bit envious of her sister. Of all of them, really. Damn, what had gotten into her tonight? Was this some kind of fall-out from what had happened in the supply closet—and Kane's subsequent rejection? She wasn't normally given to feeling sorry for herself.

"Enjoy," Marja told her. "Remember, they say men are the nicest before they say 'I do.' After that, it's all downhill."

Tania opened the front door. "Not according to our sisters and parents." She looked at her for a long moment. "What makes you suddenly such an expert? Something going on I don't know about?"

"Not a thing." Marja shook her head. "Just a matter of those that can, do. Those that can't, teach," were her parting words to Tania before she closed the apartment door.

The silence that ensued was all but deafening. With a sigh, she walked away from the door. Carelessly, she glanced at her watch. She'd called in her order to the pizza parlor on the next block about twenty minutes ago. The delivery boy should be arriving soon.

Taking her wallet out of her purse, she pulled out a twenty. The price of a small pizza and a large tip. Maybe once she finished the pizza, she'd take a ride to Queens and visit her parents, she decided. There were times when she loved having the apartment all to herself, but tonight, for some reason, she really wasn't in the mood to do anything but veg out in front of the television set. Besides, she hadn't seen her parents for about a couple of weeks.

She usually didn't let that much time go by without seeing at least one of them, not even when she was in medical school and her life had played like a tape in fast-forward mode. These days, her mother was extremely busy, getting everything prepared for the grand opening of her new restaurant. Otherwise, she knew that the woman would have been on the phone several times a day, asking her when she was going to finally come over for a visit.

That was the reason they had all conspired in the beginning to get her mother involved in running a restaurant. That, and her extraordinary skill in the kitchen. But Magda'd been a fantastic cook all her life. What had prompted this push had been Sasha and her pregnancy. They all wanted Sasha to reach term without losing her mind, and Mama had a way of overcaring, for lack of a better word.

Mama, God bless her, had a heart as big as all outdoors, but she also had a tendency to try to live all their lives for them. Because, after all, Mama knew best, Marja thought with a fond smile.

So did her dad, but at least he could be kept in line—except where their safety was involved. Then he became

Officer Pulaski, who had seen too much on the mean
streets and was determined that none of it would ever
touch his beloved family. That meant lectures and
warnings. Growing up, she would sometimes count the
months until she could move out.

Now that she had, she looked forward to going back.
Because she missed them. Absence really did make the
heart grow fonder. Once wanting nothing more than to
leave the proverbial nest, now she "flew" back whenever she had the time.

Yup, she decided, that was what she was going to do:
first have some pizza and then go visit her parents. She
knew that Tania had left the car parked in its designated
spot in the parking garage because Jesse was picking
her up tonight, so she wasn't going to need to bother
with public transportation. And since she was having
pizza, she could tell her mother that she'd already eaten.
That way maybe her mother wasn't going to force feed
her a seven-course meal.

She smiled to herself. If Mama had her way, all five
of them would have grown up round as bowling balls
and rolled from place to place.

Marja glanced down at what she was wearing. She
would have to change and put on something that was
going to afford her a little more fabric. Right now, she
was wearing ragged cut-off shorts that barely whispered along the tops of her thighs and the T-shirt she
had on was actually more of a belly shirt. She could just
hear her father. "Just because you are having a beautiful body from God does not mean that you must be
showing everyone that body."

She supposed he had a point. She was dressed like this for comfort and because the air conditioner had already cut out twice in the last week. Brown-outs were not uncommon in the summer, and outside the weather was sweltering despite the hour. Even rain brought little relief from the oppressive humidity.

She'd throw on a sundress to appease everyone. Preferably her backless sundress.

Marja was halfway to her room when she thought she heard the doorbell.

That had to be the delivery guy.

"About time," she murmured. Five more minutes and the pizza was advertised to be free. Not that she would have the heart to do that to the delivery boy. She was fairly certain the money to cover the late pizza would have to come out of his pocket.

Grabbing the money she'd laid out on the counter, Marja hurried back to the door.

"I was beginning to give up on you," she declared as she pulled the door open.

"You knew I was coming?"

Her mouth dropped open as she found herself looking up not at the face of an adolescent who was woefully in the throes of an embarrassing skin condition but at the rugged planes and carved cheekbones of the man who had all but set the supply closet on fire early this afternoon.

Kane.

Chapter 8

Marja stared at him, wondering for a moment if she was hallucinating. She then noticed that he held two pizza boxes, one small and one large.

She took a step back and opened the door wider, her invitation clear.

"Where's Mama Bear?" she asked him as she closed the door again, flipping the top lock into place. She left the chain off, hanging dormant.

Puzzled, Kane turned around. "Come again?"

Marja nodded at the two pizza boxes. "Well, you have the Baby Bear and the Papa Bear, I was just wondering where Mama Bear was." She moved closer. "I was also wondering what you were doing with two pizzas."

"I brought the big one because you said you wanted to have pizza," he reminded her. "The delivery kid at your door had this one, which I figured you had to have ordered, so I paid him for it."

Belatedly she remembered her money and thrust it out to him. "Then I owe you this."

He regarded the outstretched hand with a glare of annoyance, as if she was offering him wet dirt. "Did I ask you for any money?"

Flowers probably withered beneath that look, she thought. "No."

"Then I don't want any money." He glanced down at the boxes. The heat from the larger of the two was spreading. "Is there somewhere I can put this down? The box is hot." And that wasn't the only thing, he added silently, his eyes skimming over the skimpy outfit she had on. Right now, the woman resembled more a cheerleader than a physician.

"Right there'll be fine." Moving out of his way again, she indicated the coffee table. The next moment, he was depositing the two pizza boxes onto it. "Thank you."

He grunted something that sounded vaguely like, "You're welcome," then said more clearly, "Don't you know any better than to just open the door like that? This is New York City, not Sleepy Hollow."

She shoved the twenty into the front pocket of her cutoffs and went to the kitchen. "Now you're channeling my father," she told him, raising her voice so that he could hear her. "Besides, how do you know I didn't look through the peephole?"

He turned toward the doorway that led into the kitchen. "You didn't," he informed her in no uncertain terms. "I didn't hear it move," he added in case she wanted to argue the point. "I could have been a robber or a rapist."

"But you're not either one," she answered cheerfully. He heard a drawer opening and closing again. "And anyway, I was expecting the pizza delivery kid." Walking back in from the kitchen, her hands filled with two cans of soft drinks, paper plates, napkins and a knife and fork, she smiled up at him. "And besides, I could smell the pizza through the door."

His eyes narrowed. Now she was just making things up. "Not possible."

Hers was the face of innocence as she replied, "If you say so. By the way—" she placed the plates on the coffee table, with a napkin beside each one "—did 'busy' go away?" When he seemed confused, Marja elaborated. "You said you couldn't come over because you were busy."

Sitting down, he shrugged. "Yeah, well, it turned out that I wasn't so busy, after all."

His cell phone had been silent all evening. His brain had not. It kept reviving images of her, the sound of her voice, the way she'd looked at him when she was cleaning his wound. The way she'd taken charge in the E.R. time and again.

And the way she'd felt against him in the supply closet.

There was no way around it, he'd decided as he left the motel room an hour later. If he was going to be fully focused on his job, he needed to get something out of his blood first.

Her.

Sitting down on the sofa, Marja opened first one

box, then another. The tantalizing scent of pizza instantly escaped, filling the immediate area and leaving no salivary gland unaffected.

"What's the knife and fork for?" he asked, sitting down on the edge of the sofa, like a man ready to spring up at a moment's notice. Seeing him sit that way, she couldn't help wondering if he really did have somewhere else to be.

"For you if you want them," she answered. It only caused the furrow between his eyes to deepen. "Some people eat pizza more neatly than I do."

So saying, she leaned over and separated a piece from the large one he'd brought. She couldn't help the soft laugh that rose to her lips.

"What's so funny?" he asked.

Marja nodded at the pizza. It was completely smothered in several kinds of meats and almost an equal amount of cheeses. "This looks like a heart attack waiting to happen. They must have five pounds of different meats and cheeses on it."

"I didn't know what you liked," he mumbled into his navy-blue T-shirt.

"So you got everything." That was better than being cheap, she thought.

Kane nodded. "Pretty much." He helped himself to a healthy slice, sliding it onto his plate. A drop of sauce fell on the table and he wiped it away with the side of his thumb. "I figured it would be easier to take off than do without."

A grin spread out over her generous mouth. "A philosopher in orderly scrubs. I like that." She took a breath, diving into the pizza again. It tasted heavenly. "And I like this," she told him with relish. She saw the uneasy look in his eyes. Was he afraid she was going to be critical of his choice? No, afraid was the wrong word. Guys like Kane Dolan were never afraid. They provoked fear, didn't experience it.

She took another bite before continuing. "You only go around once, right?"

He saw a flaw in her reasoning. Or maybe he just liked to challenge her. "Then why did you order a pizza with just cheese and pepperoni?"

Her look was almost sheepish. "I was trying to be good," she confessed.

Again his eyes swept over her. Sitting down, the cutoffs were even shorter, barely covering her. "If you're trying to be good, maybe you should put on your own shorts instead of your little sister's."

"I don't have a little sister." She paused to lick the side of her index finger. She saw something akin to desire flare in his eyes. "In this family, I *am* the little sister. And you are definitely channeling my father." She sat up a little straighter, unconsciously thrusting out her chest. "Do you really want me to go and change?"

He really wanted her to shed the little she had on. But he did his best to maintain his careless facade and shrugged. "You can do whatever you like."

Her eyes smiled first, filtering it down to her lips. "I usually do," she told him. And then her eyes fluttered shut for a second as she savored another bite. "God, but this is good." Opening her eyes again, she tilted the lid on the larger box toward her and looked at the logo on the large box. "Gino's," she read. "I don't know that one," she told him, dropping the lid again.

"It's located around the corner from where I'm staying."

"'Staying'?" she repeated. "Not living?" The phraseology was telling.

Kane tried to underplay the answer to her question. He'd made a slip. Not an important one, but he didn't like that it had happened. "Trying to find someplace that fits," he told her carelessly. "Besides—" his eyes met hers "—apartments in Manhattan are expensive."

His words were met with a short laugh. "Tell me about it." She reached for a napkin, wiping the corner of her mouth. "Once Tania moves out, I'm not sure if I can afford to live here by myself."

He lowered his slice. "But you're a doctor," he pointed out.

"Last-year resident," she corrected. It would be a while before she had any practice to speak of. "The salary isn't exactly a king's ransom."

So, it wasn't as if she was going to barely be making ends meet her whole life. He knew the kind of money doctors made.

"That comes later," he told her.

She wasn't all that sure. "These days, it's the specialists who are at the top of our food chain and do well."

He already knew what each of her sister's specialized in. All that was part of the background check he'd performed on her. But when it came to Marja's field, he'd come up empty. "What specialty are you picking?"

"People," she answered glibly after a beat.

He took that for sarcasm. It surprised him. "Aren't people involved no matter what field you pick?"

"Yes, but a little more so for me." He looked cute when he was confused, she thought. And sexy, always sexy. "I'm going to be a family practitioner—an old-fashioned GP or country doctor, so to speak—sans the country, of course." Unless she set up practice in the middle of Central Park, she added silently. "I want to be the first one they come to, the one who treats their small problems and tries to help them handle the larger ones."

He took it in without showing any reaction. "Sounds demanding."

She thought of the cases that came flowing through the E.R. That was going to be what she would be up against for the next thirty-five, forty years. "It can be," she agreed.

"And not all that rewarding," he guessed.

"Not financially," she said. "But there are other reasons to become a doctor."

"I figured these days, everyone's in it for the money," he said. And that didn't just include doctors. Money made the world go 'round, whether he liked it or not.

She merely shook her head. He was obviously around the wrong people. "I need to introduce you to my sisters."

His mouth curved, but there was no humor. "The specialists."

When it came to family, she found herself on the defensive. "They're not in it for the money," she insisted. "Each one of them has a passion for the field she is in. Their focus is on helping patients, not growing rich on them."

Finished with her slice, Marja reached over for another one. The box was closer to his side of the coffee table and as she reached out, her arm brushed against his leg. She tried not to show it, but a ripple of electricity shot through her at the minor contact.

Just like a teenager in high school, she upbraided herself, annoyed with her juvenile reaction.

Watching her reach, Kane became aware that she wasn't wearing a bra beneath that abbreviated T-shirt. As she leaned forward, she'd afforded him a quick glance at her breasts, which in turn caused every fiber in his stomach to tighten. Hard.

There was just so much a man could endure before cracking.

"Maybe you'd better go and change," he told her stonily.

About to take a bite, she stopped and raised her eyes to his. "Why?"

Because I'm going to jump you in ten seconds if you don't. "Because I can only be a gentleman for so long and no longer." His eyes raked over her body. "And, Doc, you're pushing the envelope."

Her breath caught in her throat as excitement and anticipation rushed through her, pulsating. She was hardly aware of placing her slice back onto the paper plate. Her appetite had nothing to do with melted cheese and tangy tomato sauce. She had to wet her lips before answering. They'd gone desert-dry. "What makes you think I don't want that envelope delivered?"

"Careful what you wish for." Even as he said the words, Kane could feel his last barrier of restraint disappear.

"Or?" Her voice was low, seductive, gliding along his skin. Her eyes never left his, her very breath stopped moving.

Damn it, woman, I'm hanging by a thread here. "Or you might get more than you bargained for."

She raised her chin, her heart slamming so hard she thought it would break through her rib cage. "I love bargains," she whispered.

He should have never come.

He should be leaving. Getting up and walking straight to the door without another word. Without another glance.

It wasn't happening.

His knees had liquefied. He felt more powerless than the time he'd been beaten to almost a pulp in that tiny Bolivian airport. The urgent signals he sent to his body were being ignored. Instead, he could only concentrate on the magnetic pull of the extremely attractive woman to his right.

And then, something just gave way.

Kane slipped his hands around her waist and pulled her to him, his mouth sealing itself over hers.

The combustion was instant.

The preview he'd gotten in the supply closet was nothing compared to what he felt, what he tasted, what he experienced now.

Leaning back, he pulled her with him, making Marja the one to land on top. This way, he wasn't pinning her down. And, if sudden panic set in for her, she could pull back. He wouldn't try to stop her, despite the fact that he couldn't recall *ever* wanting anyone nearly as much as he wanted her.

But she didn't pull away, didn't put her hands against his chest and make a break for freedom. Instead the petite woman who'd all but set him on fire kissed him back just as intensely as he was kissing her.

Moreover, she was moving her trim, firm body all along his as if she was trying to secure a better position for herself. The resulting friction of body against body caused him to grow instantly hard. Made him instantly ready to take her.

But he didn't.

If he gave in to his own urges, if he took her now after only a few brief moments of pleasure, then he was hardly above the lowest life form. Difficult as it was, he could hold back even as he maintained contact.

He wanted this to be memorable for her. He didn't know why it mattered so much to him, but it did.

Tightening his hold on Marja, he shifted until their positions were reversed, with her beneath him and him on top. Kane drew back long enough to strip off his own T-shirt. He sent it flying into a corner. And then he leaned over, washboard abs hovering over her, and tugged away the skimpy top she had on.

Marja wriggled beneath him as she helped him pull off her T-shirt, her eyes never leaving his. His blood pounded through his veins and he bit back a groan. She looked like smoldering fire.

Desire accelerated within him like a bonfire that had gone out of control.

Again, lowering himself slowly so as not to crush her beneath his weight, Kane sealed his body to hers. For now he left her in the impossibly tiny shorts. Those would come off soon enough. He had time and waiting made the prize that much sweeter—even though it was hell, holding himself in check when all he wanted to do was plunge himself into her.

She knew it would be like this. Knew it would be like standing on the edge of a volcano, feeling the heat rise all around her, bathing every inch of her body. Knew it would be like free-falling.

And yet, it was more.

She couldn't even begin to put the sensations into words. All she knew was that she was experiencing a wondrous thrill that made her body literally beg for more. She had grown damp and she could almost physically feel the yearning. He made her want to reach the final eclipse and yet she desperately wanted to sustain this wild, erratic excitement that filled her body inside and out.

She felt insatiable.

She just couldn't seem to get enough of him, not of his mouth, not of his hands that roamed so familiarly along her body. Not of his body when he pressed against hers, firm and hard. And pulsating. She loved the way his chest felt against hers, moving against her breasts, causing the nipples to grow hard. She'd never been this aroused, never been driven this crazy with desire.

Marja sucked in her breath as his hands drifted along her lower torso, finally working away her cutoffs. She raised her hips and felt the material skim down the length of her legs. It was gone the next moment.

She wore the barest of thongs. But not for long. It seemed to vanish, replaced by the heel of his palm and then his fingers as he delved into her very center, slowly teasing the opening apart. Stroking her until she thought she was going to sob.

She twisted and gasped as she lost all control, gulping in air when she could. Wild, hot sensation burst all through her, driving her steadily up to yet another realm.

And then his hands slipped back, replaced by his mouth.

She bit down on her lower lip to keep the gasp from turning into a scream as his tongue began to probe her with movements as gentle as a whisper.

She peaked quickly, caught up in the throes of a climax. Another followed almost immediately. And then another until it all became one swirling whirlpool of sensations, of lights and colors and heat.

She was limp with exhaustion and wild with passion, all at the same time. Somewhere in the back of her head, she knew there was more, that she had to make him feel something close to what he had created for her. Even as she wanted to bask in this pleasure, she resisted because she desperately didn't want this to be all one-sided.

Summoning what little strength she had left to her, Marja gripped his arms, tugging at him. Urging him back to her level. She was vaguely aware of the way his mouth curved when he raised his head to look at her.

After a beat, his body slowly slid over hers until his face was level with hers. Parting her legs, she raised her hips in an open invitation. He needed no more.

They fit together as if they had been created that way.

Then, just as slowly as he'd proceeded before, he began to move his hips.

Tantalizing her.

Teasing her.

But his restraint was all but gone and the urgency overtook him the moment she began to move her body in time with his.

Dancing the eternal dance, they continued to increase the tempo, going faster and faster.

His fingers woven through hers, Kane sealed his mouth to hers half a heartbeat before they were both engulfed in the explosion that rocked them down to the very core of their being.

Chapter 9

Marja slowly opened her eyes as she floated back to earth. Everything inside of her seemed to grin breathlessly. As the warm blanket of euphoria receded, she could have sworn that her body still vibrated like a tuning fork.

Kane had rolled off and was lying beside her. Amazing how such a small space could accommodate them, she mused dreamily. They were two very different people. She felt like singing and he obviously preferred to retreat into silence.

Silence made her edgy.

Marja blew out a long breath. It would take awhile before her heart stopped hammering. "I should have you deliver pizza more often."

Kane didn't turn to look at her. "No, you shouldn't."

His voice was deep, solemn. Distant. Disturbing. Wedged in between the sofa's cushions at her back and the length of Kane's body on the other side of her, Marja raised herself up as best she could and looked down at his stern face.

Had she missed a step? Or was this his way of making sure she wasn't suffering under some delusion that this had meant something?

"That wasn't a marriage proposal," she told him glibly. "And I wasn't asking you to plight your troth. That was just…" And just like that, the soft, lovely feeling was gone, as if it had never existed. "Oh, I don't know what it just was."

Embarrassed, feeling like an idiot and hating it, Marja scrambled to regain her dignity and a vertical position. She climbed over Kane's inert body as quickly as possible to gather up her scattered clothing.

But she wasn't quite fast enough.

Sitting up, Kane clamped his hand around her wrist before she could make good her escape. His eyes met hers. His were flat, unfathomable. Hers, she knew, were angry. "I shouldn't have done this."

She yanked her hand away and quickly pulled on the cutoffs and her T-shirt. She still felt horribly naked. Not nude, naked. There was a huge difference.

"Why?" she snapped, zipping up the cutoffs. "Because of that caste system you have in your head? Or because there's someone waiting for you to come back tonight?"

It suddenly occurred to her that he might not be single. Kane had never said, one way or another. She'd just assumed he was alone. Was he married, engaged, *with* someone? Was this just a mindless, one-night stand, made easy by her utter willingness?

Damn, she didn't sleep around. She enjoyed sex and she tried to keep it light, but she'd never been the casual type. There'd always been feelings involved, at least on some level.

But when it came to Kane, all the rules fell apart. As if she was blindly following this pull, this surge of chemistry between them that couldn't leave her alone.

"No." It came out more like a growl than a one-syllable word, blanketing both of her suggestions. "Because I want to do it again."

All the indignation, the embarrassment, the silent upbraiding, instantly ceased. She understood now. Kane didn't like to be pinned down and he was afraid that was where this was going to go, wasn't he?

Her expression softened as the anger vanished. "I don't see that as a problem."

"You should," he told her. It was an unmistakable warning. There wasn't a hint of a smile on his lips. "You don't want to get mixed up with me."

Her mouth curved. She did her best to look strictly at his face and not at any part of his torso, but it was growing increasingly difficult.

"Too late."

He seemed utterly oblivious to the fact that he had nothing on. "No, it's not. I'm not the type to settle down."

She was right. He was afraid she was writing out wedding invitations in her head. "I don't recall asking you to."

It didn't matter if she said so or not. Things were

what they were. "Isn't that what everything is all about." It was more of a statement than a question. "Finding someone and settling down?"

Marja blinked, staring at him in disbelief. He had to be kidding. He made it sound as if it was the 1950s all over again.

"Are you caught in some kind of time warp?" she asked. "Women are pretty independent these days. They're not defined by how white their sheets come out of the washing machine or how fast they can whip up a batch of chocolate-chip cookies." Mentally, she apologized to her mother, who had always cared about the whiteness of her sheets and the quality of her desserts. But Mama was independent for all that.

"I wasn't talking about just women."

He meant women *and* men, she realized. That put a whole different spin on things. Okay, she was willing to admit that for a lot of people, love made the world go 'round and the lack thereof sometimes brought it to a skidding halt.

"Oh, well then, maybe." She moved her shoulders in a half shrug. "I suppose, for a great many people, it's about who you love and who loves you back, but finding that kind of forever love is a bonus these days." Leaning forward, she brushed hair away from his eyes. Affection skimmed through her. She did her best to make him understand that she wasn't expecting anything from him beyond the moment. "In this intense, 100-mile-an-hour world, just getting through a day is pretty big stuff."

Damn it, he wanted her again. Wanted her as much

as the first time. Maybe more. This couldn't be good. It sure as hell wasn't working out the way he'd expected. He couldn't afford to be distracted. This wasn't just about him.

He moved her hand aside. "I'd better go."

Taking a step back to give him space, she glanced down at his torso. And then smiled. The man was definitely not as disinterested as he was trying to convince her—and maybe even himself—that he was.

She thought of a song she'd once heard in one of those old musicals her mother was so partial to. "There's a really old song from the beginning of the last century, one of the lines goes 'your lips tell me no, no, but there's yes, yes in your eyes.' I think," she said, resting one knee on the edge of the sofa, her body looming over his, "that might just be applicable here."

He found himself reaching for her. With his thumb and his forefinger, he slipped the button of her cutoffs out of its hole again. Very slowly, he moved the zipper back down to its base.

"You don't know what you're getting into," he warned. This had no place to go. He had nothing to offer her. His life was rootless, that was what made him such a good operative. While she was nestled deeply in her work, in her family. Night and day. Oil and vinegar. That was them.

But he still wanted her, damn him.

"Then educate me, Kane," she whispered, lowering her face to his until her mouth was hardly an inch away from his. "Educate me," she repeated just before she sank into a kiss that reignited both of them all over again.

For a moment he let himself go, but then, against all odds, his strength of will surfaced. Kane gently pushed her back. "Damn it, woman, you make it hard to go."

"Then don't," she breathed, recapturing his mouth.

She was too sweet to resist. Kane surrendered. Just for the night, he told himself.

It was an impromptu get-together, called by her father to help soothe her mother's nerves before the big day. The opening of her restaurant, Magda's Kitchen, was swiftly approaching. The closer it came, the more convinced her mother acted that she had made a huge mistake. Or rather, her family had since they had been the ones who had talked her into this.

So the call for assembly had gone out and they had all pulled strings and traded shifts to be here for Mama. And for Dad.

"Do you know how many restaurants fail within the first year?" Marja heard her mother's raised voice demand as she let herself into her parents' tidy, two-story house. From what her father had said over the phone, Mama had been venting like this for some time now.

She followed the sound of the voices to the family room. Everyone was already there, including her brothers-in-law and Jesse. All four men prudently held their tongues.

Poor Dad, she thought, sympathizing with both her parents. Especially her mother. Despite being the personification of confidence as far as the family was concerned, Marja was certain that her mother still entertained fears of failure. It was only human.

She heard her father sigh loudly. "No, but I am sure you will be telling us."

"This is not funny, Josef," Magda declared. "This is our money I am talking about. Money you made me put into the restaurant." She wrung her hands once, then dropped them to her sides. Mama was pacing, a sure sign of her agitation. "If I fail, we will be living on the street."

"Then do not fail," Josef told her simply. "Or, if you must fail," he continued philosophically, "do it next summer. Sleeping in the street will be better then. It will be warmer."

Magda looked incensed. Natalya was quick to jump to her feet and act as a buffer between her parents. "You're not going to fail, Mama," Natalya assured her.

Kady added in her two cents, backing up her older sister. "You never fail, Mama. At anything."

Magda snorted. "Then I am overdue."

Tania changed the subject temporarily. "Speaking of overdue..." she glanced over at Sasha, sitting in the recliner, her swollen ankles raised. For six months Sasha hadn't shown and then, suddenly, she'd all but exploded. "Huge" did not begin to cover it. Tania smiled. "Aren't you?"

Magda was quick to jump on this, as well, adding it to the pile of reasons why she should have never consented to taking on this immense project.

"That is another thing." She waved her hand at her oldest child. "Who will be here for Sasha if I am standing in the kitchen, cooking for people I do not know?"

Sasha gave Tania a dark look for offering her up like a sacrificial lamb.

"We all will be," Marja told her mother, taking a seat on the floor in front of Sasha. "Besides, she'll have a whole hospital looking after her, remember?"

Magda made a small, dismissive noise, waving her hand at the words. "Who is better to look after a daughter than her mother?" Magda asked.

"No one, Mama," Marja allowed dutifully. "We'll all be just poor substitutes, but maybe between all of us, we'll equal one of you. Besides, that's the price we'll have to pay for you to become the huge success we all know that you're going to be." She turned toward her father who was hanging back on the side. "Right, Dad?"

Josef straightened. "Of course, right. It is what I have been saying. And Sasha's a good girl." He looked at his firstborn with pride. "She will find a way to have her baby when you are not working."

"I think you're giving me a wee bit too much credit here, Dad," Sasha said. She was about to say something else, but before she could open her mouth, a warning look came into her father's gray-blue eyes. They all had to placate Mama. So she offered her mother a wide smile and promised, "But I'll do my best."

Unable to stay in one place for more than a few seconds, Marja rose to her feet again. A restlessness had been coursing through her veins ever since she and Kane had made love the other night. A restlessness that had its roots in the almost overwhelming desire to make love with him again.

Banking down the feeling, she crossed to her mother

and put an arm around the small woman's shoulders. Funny, when she was a little girl, her mother had seemed like such a large presence. When had she shrunk down to this size?

"Mama, you were born to run this restaurant. You've always been a wonderful cook. It's not just our opinion. All your friends always ask you to cook for them whenever they have a party. It's time the world found out just how fantastic Magda Pulaski is in the kitchen— and time you started getting paid for your talent." She gave her mother's shoulders a squeeze. "Besides," she teased, "you signed a lease until the end of the year. You have to do something with the place, why not a restaurant?"

Magda looked at her closely. Rather than continue to dispute the wisdom of what she had gotten herself into, or give credence to what she'd just said, her mother narrowed her eyes, as if taking measure of something.

Marja could almost feel her mother's eyes boring into her.

"There is someone new, isn't there?" her mother asked out of the blue.

For a moment Marja was speechless. It had always struck her as uncanny the way her mother seemed to know whenever any one of them was involved with someone new. Sometimes Mama knew it was serious before the people involved did. Certainly before either was willing to acknowledge it. There were times, like right now, when she had the unnerving feeling that her mother had a window into a netherworld. Or, at the very least, she was psychic.

In any event, she wasn't ready to talk about this yet, especially not in a crowd scene. "I see new people every day, Mama. We all do." She gestured toward her sisters and the men who were sitting so quietly by their sides.

"I am not talking about that." Magda tilted her head, still studying her youngest child. Her eyes had become tiny slits. "I am talking about someone personal." Her mother opened her eyes wider again, looking deeply into hers. "Someone who has been personal."

It took everything she had to will the heat away from her cheeks. She knew her mother meant well, but she wished she would back off. At least until she had some kind of handle on the situation herself. Both of her parents were extremely protective. They never wanted their daughters to go through anything remotely resembling what they had personally endured while still in their native country, before democracy had been allowed to reenter the picture.

But this had nothing to do with escaping from a chaos-ridden country.

Magda's observation drew everyone's attention to her. Sasha looked sympathetic; the others, curious.

"Is she right, Marysia?" Natalya asked. "Is there someone new?"

Marja merely shrugged, hoping her sisters would pick up on the cue that she didn't want to discuss it. She didn't want to because she didn't know if there was something *to* discuss. Kane had made the earth literally move for her, but she had no idea how she had affected him or even if he would return for more.

Lord, she hoped so.

She glanced toward the group on and around the sofa. You'd think they would remember what it felt like, being under Mama's microscope, and just let the matter drop. They were here to be supportive of Mama's culinary and entrepreneurial efforts, not her divining skills.

Her sisters actually might have slipped into conspiratorial silence had Tania not suddenly looked up as if she were on the receiving end of some earth-shaking revelation. Tania caught her arm. "Oh God, it's not that guy, is it?"

"Of course it is a guy," Josef answered for his youngest. "With Marysia, it's always a guy."

"No, not 'a' guy, Dad. *The* guy," Tania corrected, then looked pointedly at Marja. "Is it?" she pressed.

"What *the* guy?" Josef asked, his father radar suddenly switched to high. He crossed his arms before him, waiting for an answer.

But instead of Marja, it was Tania who gave it to him. "The one she brought to the apartment. He was unconscious."

It sounded like a scene out of a sitcom. Kady laughed. "Can't you get a conscious one to come home with you anymore, Marja?"

"I can ask Mike to set you up with one of his friends, or better yet, one of his cousins," Natalya volunteered, then looked over her shoulder at her husband for confirmation.

Detective Mike DiPalma nodded his head. "Just say the word, Marja."

For the most part Natalya and Mike were ignored.

By everyone. Both Magda and Josef seemed keen on getting to the bottom of this mysterious man in their youngest daughter's life.

"This one she said she hit with her car," Tania volunteered. Marja glared at her, even though deep in her heart she knew that Tania was only being concerned. If the tables were turned, she would no doubt do the same thing. However, the tables weren't turned and she wasn't feeling very magnanimous right now, not when she was the subject of a Pulaski interrogation.

"Marysia, is this true?" her mother demanded. "How am I supposed to be running a restaurant if you have some kind of a problem like this? That is it," she declared like a royal monarch. "No restaurant."

"Mama, there is no problem like 'this,'" Marja assured her, siphoning the impatience she felt out of her voice. And then she sighed. "It's a long story."

Magda crossed her arms before her chest. "I am not going anywhere."

Marja knew she wasn't going anywhere, either, not until she "volunteered" the rest of the story. She did her best to summarize quickly. "He was mugged," she said in no uncertain terms. "Someone shot him and he stumbled in front of my car. What was I supposed to do? Leave him there? So I brought him home—"

Josef interrupted, obviously horrified. "You are bringing home strange men?"

"Only the ones I hit with the car," she told him wearily. "So far, he's been the only one."

"Cut to the chase," Tania pleaded. These family things

could drag on, especially when they involved their respective love lives. "Is that 'someone' in your life him?"

"What chase?" Magda asked. "We are not chasing anything."

"Except for the truth," Josef put in, his eyes shifting to Marja.

Time to wrap this up, Marja thought. "His name is Kane Dolan. He works at the hospital and we're friends, okay?"

"Maybe not so okay," Josef said. He looked over toward Byron, the son-in-law he had taken into the security firm he now ran. "But we can be having a background check on him, yes, Byron?" It wasn't a question but an assignment. An assignment Marja was determined to stop on its tracks.

"No, Byron," she was quick to veto. She appealed to her father for a little sanity. "Dad, I know you mean well, but there will be no background checks run on anyone I go out with. Not anymore." She was fairly certain there probably had been background checks in the past. Most likely, on all the men she and her sisters had ever gone out with.

Josef didn't try to argue with her. Instead he merely nodded. "Yes, dear."

"Don't use the same tone you use with Mama," Marja pleaded. Essentially, she was just being yessed but the answer was really no.

"You are using a tone on me?" Magda asked, taking offense.

"Never, Magda," Josef told her innocently. "Why do we not get back to making plans for the restaurant's

opening?" he suggested mildly. "And for now, we are
forgetting about everything else."

He didn't fool anyone.

Chapter 10

From the time when, abandoned and out on the street, he'd taken control of his life at eighteen, Kane had never had any trouble keeping his mind on his work. Even after the most vigorous of sexual encounters, he was incredibly clearheaded and focused on what needed to be done. It wasn't lovemaking to him, it was sex, pure and simple, and once it was over, it was over, relegated to a realm that rarely ever saw the light of day.

Women passed through his life and he through theirs. They were never a priority.

He moved on, the way he moved on from one day to the next. The way he'd moved on from his past. Out of sight, out of mind wasn't just a clichéd saying, for him it was reality. Nothing *ever* interfered with his work. Not because of grand ambitions, but because what he did, what he was sworn to do, was the only thing that gave meaning to his existence. Doing a good job was as necessary to him as breathing.

So it bothered him to no end when thoughts of small, supple breasts, a sleek, firm body and her smile kept infiltrating his thought processes. Like someone whose eyes moved across the page without taking in any of the words, she made his mind drift.

This wasn't why he was at Patience Memorial, to think about her, to wonder where she was as he relived the last time they were together—entirely against his will. He was here to observe, to surreptitiously collect as much information as possible about the people who worked here, and about the ins and outs of each level's floor plans, things that could never be found on a city planner's blueprints. He was supposed to be on the look out for any and all behavior that was even remotely suspicious, not concern himself with when Marja Pulaski made her appearance in the E.R.

Berating himself for his unprofessional behavior did no good. As he tried to observe the routines of orderlies, nurses and security personnel, Kane silently cursed the night she'd run into him. And cursed even more the night he'd had sex with her.

Because, while bone-jarringly good, it wasn't just sex, no matter how much he pretended it was. And that was a problem.

The hospital staff being as large and diverse as it was, with an ongoing influx of new people to replace the ones who left, was exceedingly difficult to categorize.

He could only skim the surface and remain vigilant. There wasn't enough time for anything more.

Kane relied on his instincts to guide him, his gut to warn him if something seemed out of the ordinary. That was usually not a problem. But on this assignment, his gut was entertaining other feelings, as well, receiving signals that perversely jammed his usually keen abilities to hone in on things that were out of place.

He knew he needed to purge her from his mind. A couple of times this week he actually thought he'd succeeded, only to see her hurry by, flash that smile of hers in his direction and feel himself reacting immediately, even if his expression never changed. He'd realized that he was only fooling himself. She was like a permanent marker, leaving her imprint on his very being.

He concentrated harder, worked faster and did his level best to block out as many thoughts about her as he could. In the long run, he knew that it was best for both of them. She'd weigh him down and he would only ruin her life. He had nothing to give her except a hollow shell of a man. That wasn't the type of guy she deserved to have in her life.

Kane forced himself to get busy. There were lunch trays waiting to be collected on the second floor.

"I've been looking for you."

He didn't have to turn around. He recognized her voice immediately. His back to her, he continued depositing the tray he'd just retrieved from Room 214, sliding it into one of the empty slots on the large, metal delivery cart.

"One of the orderlies on this floor called in sick."

He addressed the comment to the cart rather than her. "You've got a lull down in the E.R., so I got volunteered." The deliberately careless shrug he executed told her to connect the dots he'd provided.

A lull in the E.R. was a rare thing. In her short experience, she'd learned that, more often than not, it usually represented the calm before the storm. "It happens, every once in a while."

She was stalling, she thought. Funny, she'd always thought of herself as fearless, and yet the tips of her fingers were tingling. Nerves. There shouldn't be any and this shouldn't matter. Hell, she shouldn't even be asking. But she was. If she could ever get the words out of her mouth.

She took a breath and pushed forward, doing her best to sound nonchalant. "Are you on duty tomorrow afternoon?"

Tomorrow was Saturday. He hadn't checked to see if she was on duty, but assumed by her question that she probably was. Tomorrow morning he was meeting his handler and some of the people who were working the case. Barring something unforeseen, the afternoon belonged to him.

"No."

His answer brought a smile to her lips. "Good. Are you interested in having a good meal?"

Once social services had taken him away from Gideon and he'd finally had a sufficient amount to consume, eating never became a source of enjoyment. Eating presented the ingestion of fuel so that he could keep moving.

What he was "interested in" right now, to use her own words, Kane thought, as he watched her, had nothing to do with food.

"Are you offering to cook for me?" he guessed.

The question made her laugh. "I said, are you interested in a good meal, not are you interested in being poisoned."

The corners of his mouth curved a little in amusement. "That bad?"

"Worse," she told him. "My mother thinks the hospital gave her the wrong baby the last time around. She can't understand how someone smart enough to become a doctor can still manage to burn water."

"Interesting talent."

"Take-out places thrive on it," she assured him. Her sisters refused to let her near a stove. When it was her turn to cook, they ordered take-out. "But to get back to what I was saying, my mother's having a grand opening tomorrow—"

The wording threw him. Kane eyed her uncertainly. "Your mother's having a grand opening?" he repeated.

She'd left out the crucial part, taking it for granted that he already knew. But how could he if she hadn't told him? "Of her restaurant. Magda's Kitchen." She'd thrown the restaurant's name in for good measure.

"All right," he allowed, waiting for her to get to the point.

"Then you'll come?"

"Was that an invitation?"

She was getting ahead of herself again, hopscotching through things and assuming that her meaning was clear.

"Badly worded," she confessed, "but yes, it was an invitation."

If this was the grand opening, then there would be a lot of people there, some undoubtedly from the hospital. It afforded him a chance to mingle socially and possibly to pick up more information. But there would also be other people there. Specifically her relatives.

He looked at her for a long moment. "Is this where I meet the rest of your family?"

She heard the wary note in his voice and knew that she was losing him. The way he'd worded his question made the situation sound much too intimate, too much as if she thought she was navigating on the road to something permanent. Nothing made a guy more anxious to flee than the feel of a noose closing around his throat.

"This is where you think you've died and gone to heaven," she corrected, downplaying the part about her family being there. "My mother is one hell of a fantastic chef."

Fancy food was wasted on him. "I'm a meat and potatoes kind of guy."

"No problem," she assured him with a wink. "Just so happens that she knows how to make that, too."

It was the wink that got to him. Went straight to his gut and disarmed him without his being able to get off a single round in his own self-defense.

He moved the cart to the side, out of the center of the corridor. "You're not going to give up, are you?"

Marja didn't bother to keep her mouth from curving. "How d'you guess?"

It definitely wasn't hard. Of all the people in the hospital, she was the one he'd gotten to know best. Small wonder. "After a couple of weeks, I'm beginning to know the signs."

She laughed. "Just think what you'll learn in a month." And then, as her words came back to her, she stopped. "Sorry, didn't mean to imply that you'll be around that long."

He knew better. "Yes, you did."

She rescinded her previous statement and nodded in agreement, augmenting her transgression with another smile that went straight to his gut. The same gut that was supposed to be dead-on when it came to divining terrorist activity on the premises. The gut that kept being diverted.

"Yes, I did," she acknowledged. "You're doing a good job." Feeling partially responsible for his being at P.M., she made a point of keeping tabs on him. "God knows the nursing staff likes you and they're not always the easiest ladies to get along with." She had a suspicion that it had more to do with the man's looks than his ability to handle a bedpan.

Kane had made a point to try to get along with as much of the staff as possible, always being within earshot of any free-flowing gossip. You never knew where the most important clue would come from. The smallest, seemingly most insignificant thing could prove to be the one useful piece that could bring someone down. The serial killer, Son of Sam, was caught because of a parking ticket. Al Capone, the biggest, most bulletproof mob boss in Chicago in the thirties, was brought down and sent to prison because he didn't declare his illegal gains on his income tax form.

On the other hand, it could very well be that no insider in the hospital was helping coordinate terrorist horror. Moreover, there might not *be* anything going down and the ambassador's daughter would just have her operation and leave, safely surrounded by her father's security team.

In a perfect world.

But he had learned almost from the start that the world was definitely *not* perfect. Even though some parts of it, he thought, looking at Marja, could be perceived that way.

It might not be a bad idea to attend this thing. He might be able to pick something up, Kane told himself. "I guess I could save both of us a lot of time and effort if I just agreed to go."

"Seems like the smart thing to do." But she knew better than to count her chickens. Kane wasn't the type to just surrender if he didn't want to. She waited for the shoe to fall.

It didn't. Exactly. "How long would we have to stay?"

"Just long enough to swallow without choking." She saw him raise an eyebrow in skepticism and realized that he thought she was making an honest comment on the quality of her mother's cooking. "I meant, when you eat too fast, you're liable to choke, so—"

He held up his hand. "I get the picture. What time do you want me to pick you up?"

A sense of victory rushed through her. She allowed

herself to savor it for half a second before her thoughts turned to the fact that she was going to have to run interference between him and her family. "Then you'll go?"

"I'll go," he conceded, then added, "But I decide when I leave."

He'd said "I" not "we." Was he telling her in not-so-subtle terms that she wasn't to think of them as a couple, or was it simply that he felt he didn't have the right to tell her when to leave?

Because she was an optimist, she gave him the benefit of the doubt and went with the latter explanation.

"Deal." Marja thrust her hand out to him to seal the bargain.

After a beat, his took it in his own, shaking it. "Deal," he murmured.

Her hand in his, she felt another one of those electrical charges he was prone to creating for her zipping through her veins. No matter which way she tried to slice it, Marja thought, there was definitely *something* going on between them.

The next moment both she and Kane's cart had moved even farther to the side to get out of the way. A somber-looking delegation of five men appeared, almost all the same height and build, dressed in black suits and fitted with earpieces whose telltale coiled cords ran from their right ears to the collars of their suits. Each seemed to study the area around them as if they planned to reconstruct it upon request. There wasn't a smile to be had among them.

They had the smell of bodyguards about them, Kane

thought. Serious bodyguards. The kind that wouldn't hesitate to use lethal force if necessary.

But he played his part and asked Marja innocently, "Who's that?"

She sighed. She'd overheard one of the surgeons talking to a nurse earlier that the hospital was going to be inspected from top to bottom.

"The ambassador from Jordan's daughter is coming here for brain surgery sometime next week." The exact day and time were being kept a secret from all but the key figures involved in the surgery to cut down on the risk. "This is part of his security detail, here to check out Patience Memorial."

"Part?" he questioned innocently, wondering just how much she knew about the situation.

Marja nodded. "So I hear. Tania's been asked to be one of the three assistant surgeons and she hasn't been told when it's supposed to take place yet, just to be flexible." These days, the new, improved Tania— which is how she saw herself since she'd become engaged—liked to have everything mapped out. A nebulous fact like the surgery thrown into the mix made her crazy.

"Three assistants?" he questioned. The more people in the operating room, the greater the chance that one of them had their loyalties elsewhere. "Isn't that a little excessive?"

According to Tania, the chief of surgery had already gone over all the details and decided this was the way to proceed. "It's a very delicate operation and they'd rather err on the side of caution. Besides—and I know it sounds a little cold to say this—but witnessing this kind of surgery is a great learning opportunity for a neurosurgeon."

"Is that what your sister is?" he asked, knowing the answer already. "A neurosurgeon?"

Tania had started out wanting just to be a general surgeon. But she'd started to hone in on a specific field. Which had meant more classes, more training. Tania juggled it all.

She smiled at his question. "I think Tania wants to conquer as many fields as she can. Makes me feel as if I'm a slacker, just being content to be a family practitioner."

Is that how she saw herself? As a slacker? She was one of the hardest-working physicians he'd ever seen, handling one and a half times as many cases as any of the other doctors on duty. "Not from where I'm standing," Kane commented.

She looked at him, forgetting all about the somber men who had just turned down the corridor. "Is that a compliment, Kane?"

He heard the surprise, mingled with pleasure, in her voice.

It was a warning sign.

Too close, he was getting too close. But right now, it couldn't be helped. He really had no choice, he silently insisted. He needed the insight, the connections she afforded. Plenty of time to bail out later, after the situation was defused—if there was a situation. The chatter, according to his handler, hadn't started up again after it'd stopped.

"Just an observation," he replied matter-of-factly with a careless shrug.

She still smiled as if it was a compliment.

The next afternoon at five found him on her doorstep, ringing her bell. It was the tail end of an unproductive day and he was beat. Sometimes doing nothing was more tiring than doing something.

And then she opened the door.

He didn't know which took his breath away more, the sight of Marja in cutoffs and a skimpy top that highlighted more than it hid, or the sight of her dressed up, wearing a navy-blue, curve-hugging sheath, the hem of which was intimately flirting with the middle of her thighs.

The way his hands suddenly itched to be.

It took him a second to find his tongue. When he did, he cleared his throat. "You didn't say this was going to be formal."

The way his eyes swept over her made her feel warm. And extremely sexy. She liked feeling sexy around him. For half a second she entertained the idea of being fashionably late and bridging the time from now until then with what had so recently become her favorite indoor sport. But she'd said she'd be there early and Mama would come looking for her if she didn't show.

"It's not," she answered, "but I thought I should wear something besides my scrubs and my white lab coat. And if I went in my cutoffs, my father would throw one of the tablecloths over me so no one would see his daughter 'half without clothes,'" she said, doing a perfect imitation of her father's voice. She spread her hands out before her. "A dress was my only other option."

Grabbing her purse, she went out the door in front of him, then turned to lock it. Tania had spent last night at Jesse's and they were going to the restaurant from his apartment.

Turning around to face Kane, she let herself take full inventory. She liked what she saw.

"You clean up nicely," she told him. He was wearing a light blue shirt that he'd left open at the throat and a sports jacket that looked fairly new. Had he bought it just for the occasion? she wondered. Jeans completed the outfit and he'd managed somehow to make them look casual and formal at the same time. Not to mention very, very good.

"You, too," he murmured.

He was obviously uncomfortable with compliments from either end, receiving or giving. Kane Dolan was a very complicated man, she thought. She had a feeling that he was capable of being much more than just an orderly. What turns had his life taken to bring him there? She wanted to find out, but she knew that asking him wouldn't get her any answers.

"You know, your lips really won't fall off if you say nice things," she told him in a pseudo-confidential whisper.

He put his hand to the base of her spine, guiding her to the elevator. "I know that." When they got to the elevator, he pressed the down button on the wall. "How long did you say I had to stay?"

He was worried about being examined under a microscope, or at least definitely not looking forward to it, she amended. She had already threatened everyone in her family with bodily harm if they gave Kane even the slightest indication that they were evaluating him. She'd threatened her father twice since he and her mother were always the biggest offenders. Her mother, thank God, was going to be caught up in all the last-minute details involved in the opening.

Stepping inside the car, she slipped her arm through his. The doors sighed closed. "Not a second longer than you want to," she promised.

When she put it that way, sounding so magnani-mous, she obligated him to stay for more than a few minutes. Kane had more than a passing suspicion that she knew it, too.

Why that didn't stir feelings of rebellion or resent-ment within him, or at the very least make him angry, worried Kane.

Deeply.

Chapter 11

They took the 59th Street Bridge into Queens. Marja gave him directions from there.

After a lifetime of being frugal, her mother could not bring herself to pay the higher rental prices in Manhattan. Besides, since she'd lived in Queens ever since coming from her native Poland, she decided that Magda's Kitchen should be located in the borough, as well.

"Mama says she likes the pace better in Queens," Marja told Kane after they'd finally found a parking spot three blocks from the restaurant. Thinking of her mother, she smiled fondly as they approached the massive, wooden double doors. There were characters carved in the wood, depicting scenes from old Polish fairy tales. The doors were a labor of love from her father. "She thinks it's not quite as fast here as it is in Manhattan."

Kane nodded, not in agreement but to indicate that he'd heard her. As far as he was concerned, when it came to New York City, it was a matter of fast and faster. The word "slow" didn't really begin to depict life here.

Wrapping his hand around one of the large, solid brass handles, he yanked open the door.

Warm air and the sound of a hundred or more voices rushed up to greet them. Kane didn't like crowds as a rule—unless he was trying to lose a tail. In general, it was harder keeping track of things when there were so many variables to take into account. The fact that this was a social evening didn't really change his perception of things. He was always on his guard.

Out of the corner of his eye, he saw Marja smiling broadly, like a woman savoring a triumph. She caught him looking at her and explained, "And Mama was afraid no one would come."

He recognized a few faces from the hospital. Apparently word had gone out.

"Looks like half the borough is here," he commented. Beneath lids that appeared indolent, he quickly scanned the dining area beyond the hostess desk. It was inherent in his training. At it so long, he had no idea how to stand down. Sleeping with one eye open was second nature to him.

Several more people entered. He shifted over to one side with Marja. The group closest to him spoke in some foreign language. It sounded Slavic to his ear, although he couldn't quite place what country.

Glancing back toward him, Marja could see the somber look of concentration on his face. She guessed at the question crossing his mind. Leaning in closer to him, she said, "Polish."

"Oh." Makes sense, he thought. Her parents were Polish. Stood to reason their friends would be. "You speak it?"

Marja shook her head. "No, but I can understand it. The words don't quite come to my tongue," she explained. God knew her mother had tried, just like she'd tried to teach her to cook, but she'd always been too busy to take the time to learn. Maybe soon, she promised herself. "But I know them when I hear them. C'mon—" she grabbed his hand in hers "—let's go find the woman of the hour."

Without waiting for him to agree, she made her way through the throng like a slow-moving bullet determined to hit its target.

His first instinct was to pull his hand away, to maintain his autonomy. But he left his hand in hers and let her take the lead. Tonight was about his assignment only insofar as further establishing and maintaining his cover went.

Marja noted happily that all the tables were filled and a line of people waited to be seated. She knew most of her parents' friends and these faces weren't familiar to her. These were unsolicited customers.

Mama, I knew you could pull this off.

"Looks like your mother's grand opening is a success," Kane addressed the words to her back. She turned, apparently not hearing what he'd said, just the sound of his voice. The quizzical look on her face had him repeating his comment.

When he did, he was almost dazzled by the smile that rose to her lips. Damn, she was too beautiful for her own good. And definitely his.

The sound of the crowd all but swallowed her laugh. "She'll be successful as long as she doesn't give the food away," she told him, raising her voice. "Mama likes feeding people," she added. "Goes back to when she was a little girl. Her family was really very poor and she remembers all of them being hungry all the time."

Her mother didn't like to talk about those times, preferring to deal in the present and the future. When all of her "Doctor Daughters" as she sometimes called them, were married with children of their own.

Marja judiciously kept the last part to herself. No sense in making the man bolt yet.

They finally made it to the rear of the restaurant. She couldn't wait to see her mother. But when she pushed open the swinging double door that led into the kitchen, Marja was stunned. There was her mother, all right, moving like a whirling dervish. Nothing new about that.

But rather than a full complement of assistant chefs milling about, following Mama's orders, Marja saw her sisters, aprons spread over fashionable dresses, tending to different pots simmering on the five stoves that were lined up next to one another. Sasha's apron was stretched to the limit, vainly trying to cover her girth.

Mama was everywhere at once, issuing orders like

a seasoned drill sergeant, tasting and testing. And looking incredibly concerned.

Marja saw her father bring over a sack of potatoes and deposit it on the nearest counter, a chopping block.

"What happened?" Marja asked.

Seeing her for the first time, Josef's face brightened for a moment. "The assistant chefs, they are having trouble coming. One is sick, one had an emergency at home and one called five minutes ago. He is being in a car accident. Not hurt," he added quickly with a sigh of relief, "just being late. Oh, and a waitress is not coming, why we are not knowing."

Despite the situation, he appeared undaunted. Josef was an optimist. He had managed to escape from a communist regime with his wife. Everything after that was a gift. And if a particular moment was difficult, he merely focused on a time that would be better.

Josef gestured around the bustling area and he smiled proudly. That things wouldn't ultimately work out well never even crossed his mind. "You sisters, they are helping."

"You, too," Magda announced, all but roller-skating over to where they were standing. She thrust an apron toward her youngest daughter. "I need help with the potatoes."

Marja looked at her with dismay. She was more than willing to help, but getting her to cook wasn't going to be the answer to *anyone's* prayer. "Mama, you know I can't boil water."

Magda brushed back a strand of wayward dark hair that insisted on falling into her eyes every few minutes.

"I know you are not boiling water." Standing between her daughter and the tall stranger with her, she looked up at him, the dilemma in her kitchen placed on hold. "Hallo," she greeted as her eyes quickly took measure of him.

"Hello," he answered. Instinctively sensing that he couldn't just stand idly by, Kane asked, "What do you need?"

She eyed him, her dark eyebrows coming together over the bridge of her nose, as if perplexed by the question.

"I boil water," he explained, a slight smile curving his otherwise serious mouth.

Magda breathed a sigh of relief and grabbed both of his hands as if they had known one another forever. "Good, come. I have something for you to do."

And just like that, she whisked Kane away, for all intents and purposes, shanghaiing him.

Alarmed, uncertain, Marja quickly followed the duo. "Mama—" she began in protest.

Able to read her daughters' tones the way others read books, Magda didn't bother to turn around. "He is volunteering," was all she threw over her shoulder. "Marysia, go help your father."

In the end, it was indeed a family—and almost-family—effort that went into making the first night of business at Magda's Kitchen such a success.

There was no lull, no break in the flow, not even for a moment. Unable to assist creatively in the kitchen, Marja finally donned an apron and helped bus the tables, bringing in the dirty dishes and setting them up to go through the dishwasher. Two of her brothers-in-law and Tania's Jesse all pitched in, as well. Only Tony was missing out on the action. She didn't realize he was missing until more than half the evening had gone by.

Two of the errant assistant chefs finally showed up, but there was more than enough work to go around so her sisters and Kane continued manning the kitchen with her mother.

By the time the doors closed at eleven and the last customer had left some twenty minutes later, leaving a profusion of complimentary words in their wake, everyone was exhausted. But it was an extremely good exhausted.

One by one, as they emerged from the kitchen, they sank down at the tables closest to the swinging doors, more than a little worn around the edges.

Sasha groaned as she lowered her ever-widening girth onto a chair. The look on her face indicated she might never get up again.

Kane shifted his chair so that she might have a little more room.

Watching him, Marja couldn't begin to describe the feeling that snaked through her. She was surprised, impressed, happy, pleased and a whole host of other things flowing through her. Kane had gone above and beyond what she thought he was capable of.

She had no idea how to begin to thank him. Leaning forward, she whispered, "That was very nice of you," in his ear.

Her breath shimmied along his skin. It was all he could do to keep from shivering. Instead he shrugged off the compliment. He couldn't have explained what it was that had made him pitch in just then. Maybe because something about the older woman reminded him of his own fantasy as a boy, the one that revolved around having a mother who was a positive role model instead of the one passed out beside his equally unconscious father.

Or maybe he hated to have people come so close to their dream and not be able to grasp it through no fault of their own. It really didn't matter. He'd done what he had done and it was over.

"Needed doing," was all he said.

Magda came out of the kitchen just then, carrying a large tray before her. Her husband followed in her wake, carrying an equally large, loaded tray. The two assistant chefs brought up the rear with two more trays. All four trays had piping-hot plates of freshly made chicken à la king spread over steaming white rice.

Magda proceeded to distribute the plates to her daughters and the men with them.

"You did not eat," she reminded them. "You all came here for dinner and instead, you are working. I cannot tell you how blessed I feel to have you all in my life." She stopped by Kane, placing the plate before him. "And you, you are helping with the vegetables and I do not even know your name."

"Kane," he said, rising in his seat. "Kane Dolan." The last name burned a little on his tongue as he uttered it. Lying to the older woman seemed to bother him even more than lying to Marja.

What was that all about? he couldn't help wondering.

Resting the empty tray on the edge of the table,

Magda brushed her hand along her apron to make sure it was dry before she extended it to Kane.

"Well, Mr. Kane Dolan, I am happy to be meeting you. I am Magda and that handsome man behind me is Josef."

After working beside her all evening, it felt a little odd shaking the woman's hand as if they had just met, but Kane had a feeling that protocol was an important part in this couple's life. Nodding at Marja's father, he shook the man's hand when it was offered. Josef, he noted, had a hearty grip, as if all his feeling went into the gesture.

"We are usually more organized than this," Josef apologized, emphasizing the last part of the verb with feeling so that it came out "organize-ed."

Magda shook her head, lightly swatting at her husband's shoulder. "He is knowing this. You do not need to—"

"Mama," Sasha interjected.

Magda sighed. She didn't bother turning toward her oldest daughter. "Again someone is worrying that I am embarrassing the man—or maybe one of my daughters, too. But I speak from the heart, I am not playing any kind of games—"

"Mama." This time Sasha said the name more urgently, although it was still somewhat restrained.

Giving up, Magda turned around. She had expected Marja to try to steer her away from this new young man, not Sasha.

"What is it?" Magda cried, one hand on her hip. "Is something wrong with the dinner?" And then she stopped as she took a long look at Sasha's face. She knew that face, recognized that face. It was the same one she'd had all those years ago.

Crossing herself, she murmured, "Jesus, Mary and Sainted Joseph," under her breath, hurrying over to Sasha's side.

At the last minute Sasha's husband had been called to the scene of a homicide and had to beg off from attending the grand opening. Though he really thought it best if she just stayed home herself, Tony surrendered to her argument that she needed to be around people and who better than her family? Tony agreed that he'd join her the second he was free to do so.

Now Sasha was really glad she hadn't stayed home by herself. Although she'd attended scores of women in her condition, it just didn't take the place of being in that position herself. Giving birth alone was too scary for words.

"My water broke," Sasha told her mother unnecessarily.

The second the words were out of her mouth, all four of her sisters converged around her.

Marja took her hand. "Does it feel as if the baby's coming right away, or can you make it to the hospital?" Marja's heart hammered with excitement.

"Hospital," Sasha pleaded as a breathtaking pain overtook her and sucked her deep into its center.

"We'll take her in my car," Mike declared. Running late, he'd told Natalya that he would meet her at the restaurant and drove his police vehicle there. "I've got a siren."

Sasha stood up and the next moment her knees

buckled. She would have sunk to the floor had Kane not caught her. Without any hesitation, he picked her up in his arms, holding her as if she weighed nothing at all.

"Lead the way," he told the man he'd met over the chopping block. Mike's face was vaguely familiar and he had a feeling that he and the vice detective might have interacted at one time. But Mike gave no indication that he knew him, so at least for the time being, he was safe, Kane thought.

"It's parked two blocks over. I can pull it up to the door," Mike told him.

Kane shook his head. "Just lead the way," he repeated.

Natalya and Mike quickly took the lead. Marja fell into place beside Kane with everyone following behind. A total of eleven of them poured out onto the darkened street.

Magda stopped just short of the doorway, torn. She looked over her shoulder at what was her newest baby, the restaurant. There were tallies to make and if nothing else, it had to be locked up and secured until tomorrow came.

Reading her expression, knowing her better than he knew himself, Josef dropped back and waved her on.

"Go," he urged his wife. "I will closing the restaurant for you," he told her. "You go be with our daughter."

Magda blinked back tears that suddenly sprang to her eyes, seeming to come out of nowhere. Leaning in, she lightly brushed her lips against his cheek. "I love you, old man."

Josef smiled as if this was the first kiss they had ever exchanged. "I am knowing this. But I am not so old," he informed her. "Go, go." He waved her on again. "I will be there as soon as I can."

When she couldn't seem to get through using the cell number, Marja tried calling the precinct where her brother-in-law worked. Connecting to the dispatcher, she asked the woman to notify Tony Santini that he was probably minutes away from becoming a father.

"His wife is on the way to the hospital," Marja told the dispatcher. "Tell him to hurry if he wants to make the blessed event."

"Now," Sasha all but screamed.

"Did you get that?" Marja asked the dispatcher.

"I think Newark got that," Natalya quipped.

"Wait…until…it's…your…turn," Sasha panted.

"I think she just put a curse on you," Marja told Natalya. She tucked the cell back into her purse, turning her attention to Sasha again.

Both she and Kane were in the back seat with the pregnant woman while Natalya rode in the front with Mike. The latter was swiftly and smoothly going through all the lights. There was a lot of ground to cover between the restaurant and Our Lady of Patience Memorial Hospital in Manhattan and he aimed to set a new record.

As another colossal wave of pain came for her, Sasha grabbed both Marja and Kane's hands, squeezing hard as she tried to channel her agony through the death grip.

It wasn't working.

As the wave receded for a moment, Sasha fell back

against the seat, panting. "I always thought the first one would take its time."

Natalya responded with a short laugh. "It's half a Pulaski," she reminded her older sister. "How could you have expected it to play by the rules?"

Sasha couldn't answer her. She was being hammered by another huge contraction. They seemed to be getting larger and more devastating every time they swept over her.

In the end, they just barely made it to the hospital in time. Kady, following with Byron and her mother in the next car, called ahead to the hospital and Sasha's doctor. Sasha was one of their own and the E.R. team was waiting for her outside the hospital doors. The moment Kane lifted her onto the gurney, Sasha and Tony's baby began her journey into the world.

Sasha looked stunned as well as in agony. Marja was the first to see it. "Move it, move it, move it," she cried as she ran alongside Sasha's gurney. "She doesn't want to give birth in the parking lot."

"Where's Dr. Johnson?" Kady asked.

"En route," one of the nurses answered.

"Not good enough," Marja said. "This baby is coming."

"Not until Tony's here," Sasha cried, clenching her teeth together to keep the scream bubbling up within her in check.

Just then, they heard a car come tearing around the corner. The vehicle all but flew into the lot. It came to a teeth-jarring, screeching halt several feet away. The engine hadn't stilled yet, but Tony Santini was running toward them with the speed of an Olympic athlete being chased by a starving lion.

Thank God, Marja thought. "You can fire at will, Sasha," she told her sister.

Tony grabbed for Sasha's hand as he reached the gurney's side. They hurried her through the doors. "You okay?" he asked.

"Been…better…" Sasha cried.

Any second now, Marja thought. "Trauma room," she ordered the E.R. team. "Take her to a trauma room," she repeated.

"But the maternity ward—" the nurse began to protest.

Agreeing with Marja, Natalya shook her head. "The elevator's too far. There's not enough time."

When the orderly didn't comply fast enough, Kane elbowed him out of the way, taking possession of the gurney.

"Which one?" he asked Marja.

A quick glance told her that the closest one was free. "One," she pointed.

Natashya Magda Santini, with her father, her grandmother who couldn't be budged, and all four of her aunts in attendance, arrived less than five minutes after the door to Trauma Room 1 was closed.

Chapter 12

"It's not always like this," Marja said to Kane, finally breaking the thick silence as he drove her back to her apartment.

Her brand-new niece was now about two hours old. Natalya, the family pediatrician, had checked Natashya out and pronounced the baby to be what everybody already knew: perfect. A starry look had flared in Kady's eyes as she and Byron left the hospital. So much so Marja was certain she would probably be an aunt again approximately nine months from tonight.

Her father had arrived at the hospital an hour after the rest of them and had promptly fallen in love with his first grandchild. It had taken a total of three seconds. Maybe less. He and Mama seemed incredibly content as they left the hospital, bound for their little house in Queens where it had all started.

Tony was allowed to remain with Sasha for the rest of the night. The staff had brought in a cot for him and the new family dozed as their visitors tiptoed out of the room.

All in all, it had been a great evening for the Pulaski family, Marja thought, struggling not to get teary-eyed. But she wasn't sure how Kane had taken in what must have seemed like a three-ring circus. She told herself it didn't matter what this man thought. But she knew she was lying to herself. It mattered.

He mattered.

"My family," she said in case Kane had missed her point. "They're not always this…" Her voice trailed off as she searched for a word that was expressive but didn't come across as too judgmental. She didn't want to add to any ideas he might already be harboring.

"Intense?" he suggested.

It was too dark inside the car to read his expression. And yet he'd chosen the right word and she nodded in agreement.

"Intense," she echoed.

He slowed down for the third red light in a row. Progress was made one short block at a time. "You don't need to apologize for them."

She hadn't intended for it to sound like an apology, at least, not exactly. She just wanted him to know that while her family was an exuberant bunch, this night had been unusual. There weren't usually grand openings that needed CPR behind the scenes and babies being born.

But if he didn't think any apologies were necessary

and he wasn't intimidated or put off, why hadn't he said anything for the last ten minutes? "Then why are you being so quiet?"

He laughed shortly. "I thought a little quiet would be nice after all that commotion."

Now he was just being polite. Not that she didn't appreciate it. "You mean, noise."

Finally turning right, he spared her a glance. "If I'd meant noise, I would have said noise." The truth of it was, after he'd gotten used to the nonstop activity, he'd enjoyed himself. "Your family's a little larger than life, especially your parents." He paused, then narrowed it down even more. "Especially your mother," he emphasized.

The way he said it made her laugh. "That's a given," she told him. "Mama is fiercely protective, fiercely loyal and sometimes just plain fierce." They had all gotten used to it and loved her for her energy. But to an outsider her mother came on strong.

Kane concentrated on the road and his next red light. "You're lucky to have her."

She hadn't expected that from him. His response sounded almost intimate—and it made her smile. "Yeah, we feel that way, too, even when we're complaining about her." Grateful for the conversation, she shifted in her seat and looked at his profile. "What was your mom like?"

He didn't answer her at first. Didn't answer for so long she thought he hadn't heard the question. As they passed a streetlight, the interior of the car was briefly illuminated and she realized that his jawline was rigid.

"I don't know."

The moment he said the words, she remembered.

Remembered that he'd said something about being partially an orphan. Or rather, she'd guessed at that and he'd more or less agreed. Tired, she'd forgotten about that.

"I'm sorry," she whispered. But now that she'd stirred memories he probably preferred leaving dormant, she might as well get the rest of it. She was a firm believer that talking helped reduce the pain. "When did she die?"

He blew out a breath, debating telling her it was none of her business, then decided it no longer mattered to him anymore. "Physically or mentally?"

The sarcastic question took her aback. This was worse than she'd thought. His mother must have been the victim of an accident, sent into the depths of a coma for a length of time before she finally died. Curious though she was, she retreated. "I didn't mean to stir up bad memories."

One shoulder rose and fell in a careless response. "Not your doing," he told her. "The memories are always there somewhere, just below the surface."

His niceness made her feel guiltier. Someday she was going to learn how to keep her mouth shut. "It must have been very hard on you."

He stared straight ahead at the road, his voice distant. "I lived."

Kane retreated right before her eyes. She hated the wall that went up like a force field if she pressed the wrong button, said the wrong thing. "Yes," she said gently, "but how."

It was more of a statement than a question, a testimony to a life she couldn't begin to fathom.

While trying to imagine the kind of childhood he

must have had, it took her a moment to realize that they'd entered the underground parking structure beneath her building. Kane pulled his car up into the first available spot designated for guests. Shifting, she quickly unbuckled her seat belt and got out, then rounded the hood and came over to his side. She was afraid he would leave without a word.

Her heart ached for the boy he'd been. Opening the driver's door, she bent over, unbuckled his seat belt, then silently took his hand. She tugged gently, urging him from the vehicle.

Getting out, he was in no hurry to follow her to the elevator. If he did, complications would ensue. "Maybe I'd better go home."

Marja looked at him for a long moment, banking down the surge rushing through her body. Since they'd made love, the desire for a repeat performance was never far away. But he had to want it, too, not just go through the motions because she was throwing herself at him. "Do you want to?" she asked in a low, even voice.

"No," he told her honestly. "But maybe that's why I should."

She could understand being so overwhelmed by a feeling that she resisted having it overpower her. But she couldn't bear the idea of his being alone just now. She pictured Kane as a small boy, having to deal with a life with no mother to turn to, no mother to act as his buffer, his haven. It explained a lot of things.

"No strings, Kane," she promised. Giving voice to what was already understood between them. "No commitments." Even as she said the words, she drew him closer to the elevator. And he let himself be drawn. Into the elevator. Onto her floor. And into her apartment.

Because he wanted to.

Because he wanted her.

"What about your sister?" he asked as she closed the door behind them and slipped the chain in place.

She could feel her blood racing through her veins, her heart pounding in her chest. It all mingled into a symphony, all echoing his name. Marja dropped her purse on the floor where she stood. Her fingers got busy with the belt on his slacks.

"Tania's spending the night with Jesse." She glanced down when the button gave her trouble, working it free. "She told me so."

Her hair brushed against his throat. How could he so quickly get used to the scent of her hair, to the way her body fit against his, to the texture of her skin? How could all of that feel so familiar when he had only been with her that one time? Granted the evening had flowed into the next morning and "once" had multiplied into a number of couplings, but still, this was all new, all fresh, not something that came as naturally to him as breathing.

As naturally as taking up with the other half of his soul.

He didn't believe in souls. Didn't believe in anything he couldn't see. Feelings were not visible, he silently insisted.

But his heart raced in anticipation a second before he filled his hands with her hair and brought his mouth down on hers. Before he heard her breath get caught in her throat and felt her yielding to him, this fiery, unbendable female who had somehow woven her way into his every thought.

Desire roared through him. He ran his hands, his lips, all along her face, her throat, her breasts, each movement making him only more hungry, only more insatiable. He wanted her now, stripped of everything except her warmth.

His mouth sealed to hers as if she was the source of life-sustaining air, Kane began to tug away at Marja's dress.

The noise began somewhere in the distance, like an unheeded car alarm buzzing far away on the street. But the noise grew in volume, in insistence, and succeeded in prying them apart.

Marja was breathless. "It's your phone," she said with a barely disguised gasp as she sucked air into her lungs. He made her head spin, she thought. If he didn't make love to her very, very soon, she would wind up jumping his bones. Not lady-like, but damn necessary. "Mine has the theme song from *E.R.*," she told him.

He could feel the cell phone ringing and pulsing in his pocket. He wanted to hurl it across the room, not answer it, but he knew the former was not an option. He'd signed on the dotted line and his life was not his own. Ever.

So he yanked the cell phone out of his pocket, his brow creased with impatience. His voice was short as he barked, "Yeah?"

And then, as he listened to the voice on the other end of the call, his expression sobered. The anger and desire he felt began to recede until both had disappeared entirely.

His eyes closed, he blew out a silent, frustrated breath. "Right. I'll be right there." It sounded more like he was swearing rather than making a promise to appear.

With his thumb and forefinger, Kane snapped his cell phone closed and then pushed it back into his pocket. Tension ran through his body as he willed himself to regain control.

"I have to go," he told her. There was no room for argument, no space left where he could be persuaded otherwise.

Disappointment rolled over her. As she stood in the middle of a pool of material that had been, a few moments ago, her dress, Marja silently bent down and raised the garment back up along her hips. Never taking her eyes off his, she zipped the dress back up again. It was as if someone had thrown a switch.

The difference between the man who'd been here just a minute ago and the one here now was like fire and ice.

"Who was that?" she asked.

Nothing in his expression or manner gave him away, or gave her the slightest clue. "Just someone I know. There's a problem," he added.

Though she'd tried to hear, she couldn't discern if the caller had been a man or a woman. She hadn't been able to pick up a single sound from the other end. All she knew was that someone had called and he was leaving.

"What kind of a problem?" she asked, fairly certain that, despite the fact that they had made love, that they were going to make love just seconds ago, he wouldn't answer her question.

And she was right. "Just a problem," he responded vaguely, closing his belt buckle.

"And only you can help?" she pressed in quiet disbelief.

Was he using this as an excuse to leave? Who had called him? A friend?

A wife?

Damn, when had she started having these awful, nagging, distrustful thoughts? No strings meant no strings. For him or her. But if there were no strings, no commitment, why did she feel betrayed, cast off?

His eyes met hers. "Sounds a little conceited, doesn't it?"

He hadn't said yes, hadn't said no. Kane Dolan was very good at being evasive, she thought. At any other time, she might have even admired the ability—she'd practiced it herself often enough. But right now she couldn't, because it meant so much to her that he stay. Stay with her. Stay the night.

He was right when he'd said that it was just because he wanted to stay so much that he should be going. The sentiment went both ways. She was acutely aware that his being here meant too much to her.

It was getting too personal and nothing good could come of that.

Still, she wouldn't have been human if she didn't wonder who had him dropping everything to leave. Who meant that much to him? Who had that much power over him?

She tried again as she took the chain off the door. "Do I get a hint?"

"No."

That took the air out of her lungs again. "Well, at least you don't beat around the bush with lies."

He felt bad. He felt guilty. And most of all, he felt

frustrated as hell. Kane paused for a moment, rebuttoning the shirt that he'd almost ripped off himself. "I'll explain it to you sometime."

"But not now."

"No," he agreed. "Not now."

Very quickly, Kane brushed his lips against hers and she could have sworn she tasted a trace of reluctance in his kiss, as if he didn't want to go.

So why wasn't he staying?

And who the hell had called him at this time of night? It was closer to three o'clock than two and everything was pretty much shut down for the night.

Obviously not.

Doing her best to appear nonchalant, she flipped the lock and pulled open the door for him. "Thanks for coming to my mother's grand opening. And for helping with Sasha." She noticed that the front of his shirt bore traces of both efforts on it. "And I'll pay for the cleaning bill."

Kane looked down at the front of his shirt, then back up at her. He smiled then. Not the cynical smile or the one that seemed to hold so many secrets behind it. This one was guileless and appeared to come from the heart. "I wouldn't have missed it for the world. And no, you won't. I'll just wash it."

And then he was gone.

Marja stood staring at the back of the door long after he'd closed it behind him. The ache in her heart stilled her.

"But you're missing this," she murmured to his absent presence.

* * *

"What are you on, London time?" Kane gruffly asked the man as he slid in across from him at the last booth in the diner.

There was a cup of coffee—cold—waiting for him. The bagel next to it began to harden. Kane ignored both.

"How'd you guess?" his handler asked. When Kane made no effort to claim either the coffee or the bagel, Frank confiscated both. "Look, you knew when you volunteered that there were no regular hours. You want regular hours, go punch in as a grocery store clerk."

"To what do we owe this glowing good humor?"

Frank broke off a piece of the bagel and dipped it into the coffee to soften it. "The ambassador's daughter is coming in tomorrow."

Kane was surprised. Nothing he'd overheard had indicated that the surgery was on for tomorrow. "You're sure?"

Frank seemed affronted. "I'm sure. Her condition is getting worse," he said in a conversational tone that could have been used to talk about a street repavement program. "Her father turned the pressure up—" he rubbed his thumb and forefinger together, indicating the exchange of money "—and so the surgical team all fell into place. She's arriving first thing in the morning. *First thing*," he elaborated. "The surgery will take place almost immediately."

"Tomorrow—today," he corrected, because it was already "tomorrow," "is Sunday." For the most part, other than for emergencies brought in by ambulance, there were few surgeries performed on a Sunday.

"All the more reason to carry it out," Frank told him. He dipped more of the bagel into the coffee. "Most people won't be expecting it. The ambassador doesn't understand that even though terrorists might look like primitive single-celled beings, a lot of them at the top are damn clever. They're not taking anything at face value.

"The ambassador doesn't want to take any chances. This is his only daughter. He has more bodyguards for her than the president of the United States has Secret Service agents."

Kane stretched his legs out underneath the table. He was bone weary, but he'd get a second wind soon. "And these bodyguards, they all check out?"

Frank smiled. "Down to the fourth generation back."

Kane took in the information, nodding his head. "No chance of identity theft?"

It was an innocent question. So innocent that it had been completely overlooked. Frank's face turned an intriguing shade of purple. Obviously, he hadn't taken that little detail into account.

Instead of answering, Frank whipped out his cell phone, hit several buttons and began talking almost instantly. "Make sure everyone in the ambassador's employ is exactly who he says he is. Yes, now." He slapped the phone closed. "By the way, you're going to be there tomorrow."

He was scheduled to go in at nine as far as he knew. "At the hospital?"

Frank's eyes met his. Frank's were small, dark and unfathomable. "In the operating room."

This was news. He'd as yet not been allowed into an O.R., not even to clean up afterward. "But how…?"

Frank waved away the question. Going into details wasn't productive. "It's all been taken care of. The orderly scheduled came down with the flu."

Yeah, he bet, Kane thought. "Convenient."

Frank's smile was almost chilling. He raised the cup to his lips. "Yes, wasn't it?"

Kane sighed, already psyching himself up. Watching skilled surgeons cut open someone's skull for the purpose of operating on her brain was not his idea of fun, but, like the man said, he'd signed on for this. "Anything else I should know?"

Frank thought for a moment, then shook his head. "Just stay alert."

That, Kane thought, was a given.

Chapter 13

The moment she stepped through the hospital's electronic doors early Sunday morning, Marja noticed the difference. The electricity in the air. The tension.

As if the hospital had come under siege.

They had come, not in the dead of night, but very close to it. A small army of men in black suits, interconnected and wired for sound by virtue of the earpieces tucked into their right ears. The earpieces united them, making them a collective entity. They were like the separate cells of a body dedicated to making that body thrive.

In the case of the ambassador's hand-picked security detail, they were dedicated to the single goal of keeping both the ambassador and his beloved daughter alive during their stay at Patience Memorial.

Bodyguards were posted throughout the first floor,

where the operating room was located, as well as throughout the top floor of the tower. Yasmin would be brought to the suite after the operation, when she had made sufficient progress in the recovery room to be moved.

Rumor had it that if Ambassador Amman and the head of his privately funded security detail had their way, all hospital personnel nonessential to Yasmin's health—as well as all the patients currently occupying beds within the building—would be sent away until Yasmin was ready to leave the hospital. Barring that, both the ambassador and the head of the security detail, an unsmiling, very Middle Eastern-looking man with the unlikely, all-American first name of "Chuck," had insisted on infusing this mini-battalion into the network of people who ordinarily populated the building. Neither Patience Memorial's chief of staff, Sara Anderson, nor its current head administrator, Simon Gibbons, could oppose this invasion and still have Yasmin's operation take place here.

"I am sorry for all this," Amman had told Gibbons, "but in these dangerous times, it is necessary." The pained look on Gibbons's face bore silent testimony to the hospital administrator's reaction to the influx of black-suited men. "When your building does not blow up and your people are not taken hostage, you will find an occasion to thank me."

The simple statement clearly left the administrator, and everyone around him, wondering just what he had gotten his hospital into.

Everywhere Marja looked, preparations for the

young woman's surgery got under way. The entire hospital staff seemed involved, in one way or another. She knew for a fact that other things were going on, at least one other surgery that Kady had told her about. But Yasmin's surgery seemed to take precedence.

It was like being caught up in a tape where someone had pressed Fast Forward and forgotten where the Play button was. She couldn't recall ever seeing this many people milling around on the ground floor.

It wasn't easy finding Kane amid this throng. But that was why she'd come in before her shift. Last night's abrupt departure was still on her mind, still bothered her. There was more going on with him than met the eye and she wanted to know what. More than that, she wanted to know what she was getting herself into before it was too late.

If it wasn't already, she amended silently.

She'd gotten very little sleep the remainder of the night, waiting for him to call her, annoyed with him— and herself for caring—when he didn't.

Had he used the phone call as a convenient excuse to leave? After all, she had no idea who had been on the other end of the line, or what they had said. For all she knew, it could have been a wrong number and Kane had used it to make good his escape. Had her exuberant family frightened him off?

She kept telling herself that it didn't matter, that she didn't really care, but that was a lie. It *did* matter and she really *did* care. Enough so that after giving him the benefit of the doubt over and over again until dawn, she wanted to hear the truth from his own lips.

They needed to talk.

She wasn't expecting a detailed map telling her where she stood with him, but she did want to know if her feet were planted on solid ground or quicksand.

When Marja finally spotted Kane, he was on his way to the side of the building where the operating rooms were located. He seemed to be in as much of a hurry as everyone else.

Too bad, she thought. He could spare her five minutes.

She picked up her pace and hurried after him. It wasn't easy. He had almost ten inches on her and it seemed to be all leg. She was practically trotting at the end.

Finally managing to catch up, Marja began, "About last night—" a line that she was well aware had a special place in the Cliché Hall of Fame. She wasn't allowed to go any further.

"I should have called," he told her, simultaneously taking the blame and the air out of her sails. He didn't even seem surprised to see her and he was talking faster than she'd ever heard him talk before. She wouldn't have pictured him as someone who could get caught up in what was going on. He didn't seem like the type to dance to anyone else's tune. "But right now, I've got to get into that operating room."

"That" operating room was the one where Yasmin Amman's operation was to take place. Was he crazy?

Marja caught his arm, stopping him from going any farther. "You're liable to get killed. They're not going to just let you waltz in."

Very deliberately, he removed her hand from his arm. He saw concern in her eyes and, against his will, she got to him. He couldn't remember the last time anyone had been concerned about his actual well-being, apart from getting the mission accomplished.

"You don't understand," he said patiently. "Ecklund told me to be there."

She stared at him, stunned. "The neurosurgeon in charge of organizing the surgical teams told you to be there?" She was obviously missing something. Kane didn't strike her as someone who would give himself false airs, and yet she didn't see him and Dr. Aaron Ecklund even remotely moving around in the same circles.

But Kane merely nodded in response to her question. "And if I don't hurry, I'm going to be late." He picked up his pace, leaving her behind.

Marja's mouth dropped open as she watched Kane approach one of the two men standing guard outside Operating Room 1, the largest of the five available operating salons.

Holding up his laminated ID for the guard to view, Kane waited while the burly man went down the list of specified hospital personnel allowed into the operating room. The guard perused the list slowly. Coming to a name that matched the one on the ID, the guard placed a large, black check next to it, looked once more at the ID Kane extended toward him, then finally nodded his approval.

"Go in," he said in a voice that seemed to be coming from somewhere deep in the Grand Canyon.

Kane slipped in between the two doors, leaving her standing out in the corridor. Marja felt as if she were rooted to the spot.

"Move along, please."

The entreaty, directed toward her, was politely worded. There wasn't the slightest doubt in her mind that if she opposed it, or attempted to resist, the man could and would physically remove her.

What the hell was going on? she wondered as she retreated, slowly walking back to the E.R.

Her shift didn't officially begin for another half hour. Instead of being able to talk to Kane and hopefully resolve what was—or wasn't—going on between them, she'd been confronted with disjointed pieces of a puzzle.

Kane had only been with the hospital a little more than three weeks. Most orderlies weren't allowed into the O.R. for clean-up purposes *after* a surgery had taken place, until they'd been at P.M. for at least a couple of months.

Something was definitely out of kilter, she thought, chewing on her lower lip. And she intended to find out what.

Periodically, whenever she had a break, or there was a lull in human traffic, Marja would venture out into the corridor and quickly make her way toward O.R. 1.

The scene never varied.

Thanks to Security, there was a minimum of foot traffic near the area. The same two big, burly sentries she'd seen earlier were standing guard, each with one of the two doors at his back. To the passing eye, they looked like two statues painted in flesh tones to make them appear more human. A measure that just barely succeeded. Had she not seen one of the men checking Kane out before he'd gone in, she would have been convinced the bodyguards were made of marble.

The surgery was scheduled for six hours. It ran longer, stopping the clock at nearly eight. As each hour passed, the tension around the hospital, especially the first floor, seemed to grow.

Instead of taking a lunch break, Marja decided to pop in on Sasha on the maternity floor. Although most of the floor was empty, because a large number of mothers had checked out with their little bundles of joy just prior to noon for insurance purposes, the area around Sasha's bed was incredibly crowded.

So many people were there, Marja felt as if she should have taken a number.

"Hey, what about the 'two to a bed' rule?" she teased, wiggling into the room designated as a single-care unit rather than "private," a label that was a health insurance taboo. Between visiting family members, hospital staff and extraneous police detectives, there really wasn't much space available.

"Never heard of it," Tony deadpanned.

Tony was currently holding the baby. The tiny bundle had quickly learned to accept being handed off from one set of arms to another.

"She likes all the attention," Sasha told her proudly when she made eye contact with her older sister. "I think I've given birth to a social butterfly."

"That she gets from me," Josef said proudly.

Mama responded with something very close to, "Ha!"

Marja burrowed in beside Sasha. Despite the wide

smile, Sasha seemed exhausted, although better than last night. "How are you feeling?"

"Like a truck ran over me," Sasha confessed. "But it was a nice truck that dropped off a very precious bundle," she added, beaming at her husband holding their daughter.

Marja scanned the gathering. With all the people packed into the room, there was hardly any space for a sneeze to fit in. "Well, no failure to bond here," she quipped.

Josef picked the same time to examine the faces in the room. He came up one short. "Where is Tania?" he asked. "I would be expecting her to be here."

"Tania's in the operating room," Marja told him before she could think better of it.

An alarmed look came into Kady's eyes as she made contact with Marja. Standing behind her parents, she still had on the scrubs she'd worn while observing another last-minute operation. Kady shook her head. But it was too late for warnings.

"Which one?" Josef asked, the smile disappearing from his face.

She'd blown it, Marja thought. There was no sense in worrying her parents needlessly. "I'm not sure."

Tufted eyebrows joined together above gray-blue eyes. "Lying to me you were never good at," he admonished. "It is the operating room with Ambassador Amman's daughter, is it not?"

Magda's attention was focused on her youngest child. "Is she in danger?" she asked urgently.

"She's fine, Mama," Natalya insisted, covertly giving Marja a dirty look. "It's a great learning experience for her. Aaron Ecklund is an incredibly gifted neurosurgeon. This is an opportunity of a lifetime."

Coming between her parents, Marja slipped one of her arms through each of theirs as if to make plans for a picnic, not talk about a life-and-death surgery.

"Everything is fine," she assured them. "When are you two going to stop worrying?"

Magda never hesitated. "When we are dead. Not a minute before." And then she smiled, gently passing on the legendary "Mother's Curse." "Wait until you have children of your own, you will see."

"Children of her own." Josef laughed, shaking his head. "We should only live that long."

But he was smiling as he said it and, for the moment, the tension in the room disappeared.

It was over.

The operation, the recovery, all over.

Ninety minutes after surgery was completed and deemed an overwhelming success, tissues from the tumor being rushed into the lab for a biopsy, an unconscious Yasmin Amman, with her father in attendance, was wheeled out of recovery and up to her tower suite.

And Kane was the one doing the wheeling—along with a nurse, the ambassador's personal physician and two of the bodyguards. Counting Amman, it made for a more than full elevator.

Kane looked down at Yasmin's sleeping face. The ambassador's daughter had survived the surgery, and so had the hospital, he thought.

But he was not about to celebrate yet. There were

still a multitude of hours left before the young woman could be checked out of the hospital and on her way home again. Once she was discharged and physically out of the building, his responsibilities were at an end. She would be someone else's headache then. He had only been charged with dismantling any terrorist activity aimed at her—or the hospital—while she was staying at Patience Memorial.

Kane took heart in the fact that Amman was anxious to fly his only daughter back home in his personal jet at the very first opportunity.

Opportunity would be knocking in approximately three days.

Modern science was incredible, Kane thought. There was a time when a simple tonsillectomy would have kept a patient confined to a hospital bed for a week. Now they all but catapulted you out of the hospital practically the second the anesthesia wore off.

But that still left him three days in which to remain vigilant 24/7.

There was a security guard posted before Yasmin's room, standing watch over the empty suite in her absence. The man looked like a carbon copy of the two who had accompanied Yasmin up in the elevator. Someone should do something about the design, Kane thought, lightening up a little.

It went without saying that no one was allowed into Yasmin's room, even when she wasn't there, without proper supervision.

They certainly knew how to guard their own, Kane thought.

He felt superfluous in his present role, but then he supposed that was a good thing. Better than the alternative, to be needed everywhere at once and run the risk of overlooking something. Something that might prove deadly.

"Want to get that?" he asked the guard closest to him, nodding at the door. The hulking man pushed it open with the flat of his hamlike hand.

Entering the room under the watchful gaze of not just one but all three bodyguards, Kane then proceeded to help transfer the unconscious young woman from the surgical gurney to her bed. She moaned, but mercifully continued sleeping.

Kane went to physically adjust the rack holding Yasmin's IV drip, only to be moved out of the way by the ambassador's personal physician, a tall man with twice his share of hair and wide shoulders. The physician could have easily substituted for one of the bodyguards.

"I will take care of that," the doctor informed him in a voice that only had a slight trace of an accent.

Kane obligingly backed away without a word. But he did watch the doctor make the adjustments—as did the two bodyguards in the room.

All checks and balances, Kane thought. Nobody trusted anyone else and they weren't out of the woods yet. Maybe they never would be, he thought, putting himself in the ambassador's shoes. Death threats aimed at him and at his family were a way of life.

Now that Yasmin was transferred and in her own bed, Kane pulled the sheet off the gurney, bundling it up. Pushing the gurney out the door again, under the brooding gaze of at least one of the bodyguards, he almost ran into another orderly.

The latter was pushing a large laundry cart before him, collecting soiled linens from each of the suites. It was something that went on daily as nurses and orderlies stripped off yesterday's bed linens and replaced them with fresh ones.

The orderly looked at the wadded-up sheet on the gurney. "I'll take that off your hands," he offered, putting out his hand.

"Knock yourself out," Kane murmured, transferring the sheet to the other man. He quickly glanced at the orderly's name tag. John. It rang no bells. Nice and anonymous, he couldn't help thinking.

Dumping this newest acquisition into the already filled laundry cart, John nodded at him and then struggled to make a U-turn. Yasmin's suite was the last one on the floor.

The cart wasn't cooperating.

"Need help?" Kane offered.

John shook his head. "Nah, got it covered." Each syllable he uttered was encrusted with a thick, Brooklynese accent.

Kane merely nodded, turning his gurney toward the elevator. He needed to get rid of the gurney and either find an excuse to come back, or hang around discreetly. He preferred the former.

Out of the corner of his eye, he saw the orderly proceed on to the next room, another suite, although not quite as large as the one Yasmin and her entourage occupied. This time, rather than remain outside, since there were no guards posted, John disappeared into the suite, pushing the laundry cart in front of him.

He was out again almost immediately, more linens piled up in his cart. Instead of struggling with it, he easily pushed the cart toward the elevator.

Something didn't feel right.

Maybe it was his need to keep active, Kane thought. Or maybe it was his way of dealing with last night—or not dealing with it. But something was out of order in the universe and right now it centered around the laundry cart.

He watched the orderly's progress down the hall and to the elevator. The suite next to Yasmin's had been his last stop.

Was it his imagination, or was the cart rolling better now than it had been when John had attempted to make it turn around?

And if it was rolling better now, why?

Crossing to the elevator, he nodded at John, one orderly to another in the midst of strangers. "Lots of excitement today, huh?"

John stared straight ahead at the stainless-steel doors. "Yeah."

Striking up conversations was not his forte, but he did his best. "They just hired you?" he asked. "You don't look familiar."

John shrugged. "Last Monday," he mumbled. "They got me doing laundry."

"I see that. Hey," he suddenly cried, splaying his fingers out around his neck. "It's missing," he said as if talking to himself. Then his eyes darted toward the laundry cart. "You think it fell in there?"

"What fell in there?" John asked defensively.

"My cross. I had it on when I stripped the gurney. Maybe it got caught in the sheet and I tossed it in there." Kane peered into the cart. "My wife'll kill me if I lose it."

Not waiting for permission, he began moving the dirty laundry around, digging his way toward the bottom of the cart like a man in search of something.

But there was nothing in the cart except for dirty linens and damp hand towels.

"Must've lost it somewhere else," the orderly told him just as the elevator arrived and opened its doors.

Kane stepped back, not getting on. He nodded behind him. "Maybe I'll look around, see if it fell off in the suite."

"Yeah, try that," John agreed as the doors closed.

Kane turned around to find Marja standing right behind him. The expression on her face was one of devastation. And disappointment.

Chapter 14

"Your wife?" Marja cried in disbelief.

Oh, dear God, she'd slept with a married man. Worse, she'd let herself have feelings for a married man. Feelings? Hell, she was in love with the bastard. The realization shook her down to her very toes. How could he have lied like that to her?

"You have a wife?" she demanded.

"No," Kane said tersely. He didn't have time for this now.

He looked toward the last room the orderly with the cart had gone into. Kane couldn't shake the feeling that something was off.

Why had the cart wheels been squeezing and groaning one minute, then whizzing along the next? Since he hadn't found anything in the cart, there was only one explanation. The orderly had left something in the last suite. Something fairly heavy.

He was ignoring her. She damn well wasn't going to let him. She'd come up here, looking for him and he was going to explain himself even if she had to squeeze it out of him.

"But I heard you say to the orderly—"

Again he cut her off. "Long story. I'll explain later."

"You'll explain now," she told him, her voice deadly still.

She didn't usually take stands or draw lines in the sand with the men she dated. She hadn't cared enough for that. Sharing their company was all free and easy. Nothing really serious.

But from the moment she'd set eyes on Kane, she'd known this was going to be different. That this man was different. Good different or bad different, she wasn't sure—although it seemed to be tilting toward the latter at the moment—but this man mattered.

This man, even as she tried to deny it, was going to hurt her if she let him.

If?

She'd already let him. And it already hurt.

Kane made no answer. Instead he crossed toward the suite that was right next to Ambassador Amman's daughter's room.

Not about to be left behind like an old toy, Marja followed quickly in his wake.

"Are you even listening to me?" she demanded.

He stopped abruptly and turned toward her. "Whose room is this?"

"Obviously not." She answered her own question. She thought for a second to answer his. "It's Amin Sayid's room." There was recognition in Kane's eyes. The man read the newspaper, she thought sarcastically, her feelings still smarting. "He's the head of an international banking firm, domiciled in Saudi Arabia, currently friendly toward the U.S. I forget the name of the bank." She blew out an impatient breath. "What does that have to do with anything?" she asked.

It hit Kane like a streak of lightning. They'd been wrong, he realized. The target wasn't the ambassador's daughter. It was this man, the banking CEO. It had to be. It was all beginning to make sense. The chatter about the daughter had been to throw them off. The terrorists were going to make the CEO pay for allowing his company to do business with an enemy nation.

"What are you doing?" Marja demanded.

Kane didn't answer. Instead he pushed open the door to Sayid's suite and walked into the room, quickly scanning the length and breadth of it. There was no one there except for the patient.

The banking magnate, small, fragile-looking and as far away from appearing to be a dynamic man as possible, was asleep. There was an IV drip attached to his arm. Monitors beside him were hooked up to his chest, bearing witness to the fact that his vital signs, although weak, were all stable.

There was a chart at the edge of his bed, but Kane had no time for reading. Instead he looked to Marja for answers. "What's he in for?"

"He just had an operation, too." Ordinarily she wouldn't have known, but Kady had mentioned she wanted to sit in on the operation and observe. "A shunt in his heart. Why are you asking these questions?" Moving around her, Kane handled the IV tube. "And what are you doing?" she demanded. He had no business handling the IV.

Damn if he could tell if anything was wrong, he thought in frustration. He had no choice but to get her to help him. "Can you see if there's anything wrong with the IV?"

He wasn't making any sense. "Why should there be anything wrong with the IV?"

"Please," he insisted. "Just check it out."

Muttering a few choice words under her breath, Marja gave the IV line a quick once-over to see if it was correctly hooked up, that there was no danger of an air bubble getting in the line and terminating the man's life.

"Who are you?" she asked.

When he made no answer, Marja pulled out her cell phone to call Security. She yanked too hard. It slipped out of her hand and fell on the floor. Hitting the carpet, it bounced sideways, landing just under the bed. No longer quite sure what Kane was capable of, she quickly scrambled to pick up the phone and make her call.

On her knees, Marja reached under the bed for the phone. And then froze. "What is this?"

Kane had just checked the closet and was about to open the bathroom door when he heard her. She'd found something. Hurrying back to the bed, Kane dropped to his knees.

He saw what she saw.

Except that he knew what it was.

"Damn." He swallowed a more colorful curse. There wasn't time to vent. He had no idea how much time they had. His heart felt like lead in his chest. "Get out of here," he ordered.

Marja looked at him from beneath the other side of the bed. "What?"

"You heard me!" He rose to his feet and hurried around the bed to her side. "Get out of here!" Grabbing her by the arm, he began to pull her to her feet, but she yanked free of his hold and stubbornly remained on her knees. "Call Security and tell them to evacuate the floor. And get this guy on another bed!"

Her mouth instantly went dry. Still on her knees, she sank back on her heels and looked up at him. This was all beginning to sound surreal. "Who *are* you?" she repeated.

"Somebody who knows a C-4 bomb when he sees one." This time he grabbed her by the shoulders and succeeded in pulling her up to her feet. "Give Security a description of the orderly who just left with the laundry cart. Tell them to find him and hold him. A lot of lives may depend on it."

Definitely surreal. She forced herself to focus. "You think he did this?"

"I don't know," he told her honestly. "But he's involved somehow. Now go!"

She didn't budge. She wasn't about to leave him here if there was a bomb in the room. "Why aren't you coming with me?"

The answer was very simple. "Because somebody's got to take this thing apart."

Her eyes widened with horror. "But what if it takes you apart?"

"Don't argue," he ordered.

"And don't move."

The last order came from the small, wiry man emerging out of the bathroom. He was smiling, displaying a row of dazzling white teeth. His smile was as cold as the steel of the gun that he held aimed at Kane.

"No one is going anywhere," he said with finality. "Unless I say so. Now, get over by the wall. Slowly." The man in orderly scrubs waved his gun, indicating where he wanted Kane to go.

In all the excitement, Marja had sunk down to her knees again. Kane looked at her, concerned. If she wasn't in the room, no doubt he would have tried to wrench the weapon away from the other man. But she was here and the gun could very easily discharge and hit her. He couldn't take that chance.

So he did as he was told, backing up as he waited for the proper moment to try to take the man down.

Dark, steely eyes shifted toward Marja. "Get up!" the orderly commanded, all traces of the cold smile vanishing.

Marja shook her head. She did her best to look disoriented. Feigning fear was not as difficult.

"I can't. I feel dizzy," she cried. "My knees are weak."

The dark-haired orderly loomed over her, his eyes narrowing into hate-filled slits. "Pathetic weakling. Our women have more courage."

Marja didn't say a word. Instead she fell forward, appearing to faint. Kane cursed and took a step forward to help her.

The terrorist cocked his gun. "Stay where you are," he warned. And then he screamed in pain.

Marja had driven a syringe into his ankle.

The distraction was all Kane needed. Grabbing the terrorist from behind, Kane wrapped his arm around the man's throat, applying enough pressure on his windpipe to cause him to pass out.

When Kane looked toward Marja, he grinned. There was admiration in his eyes. "Not bad for a civilian," he commented.

Civilian. Which meant what? Who was this man? she wondered for the umpteenth time.

On her feet, Marja quickly called hospital security, identified herself and rattled off all the instructions Kane had given her.

Breathing a shaky sigh of relief, she slipped the phone back into her pocket. She knew they weren't out of the woods by a very long shot. She watched as Kane quickly tied up the other man. She was willing to bet he hadn't learned how to make knots like that in the Boy Scouts.

The international banking CEO continued sleeping in his bed, oblivious to the drama going on around him.

Marja looked toward the bed, her heart still hammering wildly. "Why aren't you trying to disarm the bomb?" she asked, amazed at how calm she sounded asking the surreal question.

Finished tying up the orderly, Kane removed the cell

phone clipped to the waistband of the man's scrubs. "Not until you get out of here."

"Well, then we have a problem because I'm not leaving you," she informed him.

This was no time for a battle of wills. "Yes, you are."

She put her hands on her hips. No way was she going to leave. "No, I'm not," she enunciated very slowly. "You might not know this, but Polish women are exceptionally stubborn."

"No games, Marja." Buffering her shoulders with his hands, he stared into her eyes. "I'm not going to be able to concentrate if I have to worry about you—and I will worry about you if you're not outside the building—somewhere safe."

Oh damn him, anyway. Marja struggled to keep the tears back. "That's possibly the nicest thing you've ever said to me under the worst possible conditions."

"Nothing's perfect," he said philosophically. Releasing her, he gave her a little push toward the door. "Now get out of here."

Marja was torn, but she also knew he was right. She couldn't take a chance that he wouldn't be at the top of his game. Any kind of distraction would be fatal, to him, to her and to whoever hadn't cleared out if the bomb should go off.

But she really, really didn't want to leave him at a time like this.

"Damn it, make sure you do it right," she told him, tears coming into her eyes. "One of you is hard enough to deal with. I can't handle the thought of you in a thousand pieces."

"No pieces," he promised as if it was entirely up to him. But these sorts of bombs were operated by remote control, not timers. He needed to separate the C-4 from its detonator before someone had a chance to make the fatal call. If luck was with him, the phone he'd just confiscated from the pseudo orderly was the one whose frequency was wired into the bomb. But he couldn't count on it.

Marja took him by surprise. She kissed him. Hard. "I'll hold you to that," she threatened. Knowing she had to leave, she wanted to say one more thing to him. One more thing she might not get the chance to say to him later. "I love you."

Kane stared at her, stunned. The next moment the room was invaded not just by the hospital's security personnel, but the other men on his team. Marja was surprised as she recognized two of the three other men who came in.

"Did you check his pockets for a cell phone?" Marcus Montgomery, the tallest of the three men, asked Kane.

Kane held up the phone in his hand, surrendering it to Montgomery. "I don't think that's going to set it off. He didn't stay behind to set off the bomb. I think he was here to make sure that nothing interfered with the plan."

Montgomery shook his head, contempt in his brown eyes. "Another suicide fanatic."

"Wake him up and see if you can get anything out of him," Kane ordered. Turning to the other two men on his team, he continued to rattle off instructions. "Call the bomb squad. Evacuate this floor and the rest of the tower. If we're lucky, that's all the bomb'll take out if it blows."

Finished, Kane dropped to his knees and then slid under the bed.

"What about you?" Montgomery asked, bending down to look at Kane.

"I'm going to be busy sweating," Kane answered. "Now get the hell out of here and take everyone else in the room with you."

The room was not clearing as fast as he would have liked. He could still see several pairs of legs from his vantage point. "Move, people," he ordered. "Now. This means you, too, Marja."

"Not until I get the patient out," she answered. There was a hitch in her voice. "I might not be able to get you to go, but I'm not leaving without him."

The next moment he heard the door being opened again and saw the bottom of the gurney that he'd left out in the hallway, the one that had been used to wheel Yasmin in. Kane was feeling antsy.

"Hurry it up, people. We don't know how much time we have left."

"On my count," he heard Marja say after lining the gurney up next to the bed.

"Don't count, *do,*" Kane ordered.

The bed shifted slightly as the unconscious CEO was moved onto the gurney. His eyes were glued to the bomb that resembled a glob of extra-large Silly Putty with wires running through it. Kane held his breath as the bed frame, depleted of the extra weight, rose a hair's breadth higher.

Nothing happened, other than sweat drenching him.

Within a few scant moments, the security men all re-

treated from the room. Two members of his team removed the unconscious terrorist, dragging the man between them. Listening, he heard the door closing. "You,
too, Marja."

Only silence met his words.

"Marja, I mean it. I'm not working on this until you
leave. Now."

He heard her sigh. "How did you know?"

"The security guards don't wear perfume." And his
nose had grown exceedingly sensitive to the scent.
"Now, go."

"Be careful," she admonished, feeling like an idiot
because the words felt so useless.

"I'll do my best," he answered.

When the door closed again, silence settled into the
suite. All Kane could hear was the sound of his own
breathing and the hammering of his heart. He wondered
how fast the bomb squad would be and if there really
was enough time for them to get here. Like other agents
in this line of work, he'd been trained on how to dismantle a bomb, but he'd only done it twice in the field.

He couldn't help wondering if his luck would hold
for a third time, or if, with the third time, the bomb
would win instead.

Flexing his fingers, it occurred to him that they felt
unusually stiff.

Kane took a deep breath. No time like the present to
find out if he or the bomb would come out on top.

There wasn't any time to worry. Rather than run to
the elevators to seek the shelter Kane had ordered her

to take, Marja hurried to Yasmin's suite. The body-guards posted outside her door, alerted by the commotion down the hall, were instantly ready to take down anyone who breeched their space. Marja found herself looking down the barrel of a very complex piece of hardware she assumed was a state-of-the-art gun.

"We need to evacuate the floor," she told the man who stepped forward, his steely eyes silently warning her back. "There's a bomb in the next room."

The bodyguards looked at her for a long moment, as if trying to decide whether she was telling the truth or wanting to harm the two people they were sworn to protect.

Damn it, there wasn't time for this contest of wills. "Look, it's liable to go off any second." The words formed a huge lump in her throat as she thought of Kane in the other room. She pushed past it. "So if you want to save that young woman in there, you'll help us get her out of here."

When they wanted to, the ambassador's security detail could move very quickly, despite their bulk. Rather than search for a gurney, the bodyguards pushed the hospital bed into the elevator. Marja went down with them, but before she got into the elevator, she smashed the glass on the fire alarm and activated it. She was counting on that to get everyone moving.

Prepared for any sort of crisis ever since 9/11, the hospital staff evacuated the building even as sirens screamed above the usual city din, announcing the arrival of the bomb squad and still more police personnel.

After she was certain that the ambassador's daughter was safely on her way to the first floor, Marja got out on the fifth floor and rushed to Sasha's room. Technically, according to Kane, everyone outside the tower was safe. But what if he was wrong?

Better safe than sorry, she thought.

When she got off on the maternity floor, Marja found herself all but swimming against the tide of nurses. Every one of them was wearing a baby apron designed to help carry out four babies at the same time, each secured in what amounted to a special deep, wide "pocket." Luckily, there weren't that many babies left on the floor.

"Marja, what's going on?" Sasha asked when she burst into the room, pushing a wheelchair that she'd commandeered in front of her. "Is there a fire?"

"No, no fire." She scooped up her niece, who was in the bassinette by Sasha's bed, and placed the baby in her sister's arms.

"Then what?" Sasha asked.

Lining up the wheelchair next to the bed, she took the baby back for a moment. "Get into the wheelchair," she ordered. Holding Natashya against her with one arm, she used her other hand to help guide Sasha. Her sister was still very weak.

"But what's going on?" Sasha asked.

Marja tucked the baby back into her arms. "I'll explain later."

She realized she'd just said the same thing Kane had said to her when she'd asked him for an explanation.

It sounded better coming from her, she thought stubbornly.

"Okay, here we go," Marja announced. "Brace yourself, Sash, it's a little crazy out there."

It was a vast understatement, but because of all their training, the staff managed to avoid pandemonium.

Still, Marja couldn't avoid feeling anxious and deeply worried as she guided her sister's wheelchair onto the freight elevator.

Kane was still up there.

Chapter 15

It was taking too long. Why wasn't he down here yet? Something was wrong.

The three short sentences kept dancing through Marja's brain, shuffling over and over again like cards with no game to play.

Her stomach was in knots.

Marja had deliberately placed herself at the hospital's main entrance, where she could see everyone as they evacuated the building. None of the people coming out of the hospital was Kane.

The mix of people filling up the front parking lot was diverse. Along with patients, aided by hospital staff members, there was the police department, the bomb squad and reporters from every single news station and paper in the tristate area. Not to mention the firefighters who had come in response to the fire alarm she'd pulled. And then there were the bodyguards, surrounding the ambassador and a sleeping Yasmin like a human wall.

Everyone was present and accounted for except Kane.

Now that she was down here, her mind created horrible scenarios. A sense of restlessness pervaded her.

She couldn't stand it any longer.

She had to go back up to see why Kane hadn't come down yet.

Marja glanced over her shoulder. For one second she debated saying something to one of her sisters, all three of whom were clustered around Sasha. Tony had heard the bulletin over the radio in his police car and had instantly doubled back to the hospital. He'd just found them a few minutes ago. Most likely, if she knew them, her parents were on their way in, as well.

If she told any of them what she intended, they'd inform her that she'd lost her mind and physically restrain her. Just as she would if it was any of them who wanted to go back in an unsafe building.

But it wasn't any of them, it was her. And Kane.

So, without another word, she quietly slipped away and wove through the crowd until she reached the side of the building. Making sure no one official saw her, she darted in through the door ordinarily used by X-ray technicians as a private exit. It was located directly opposite one of the hospital's three stairwells.

Once inside, she breathed a sigh of relief. Any remaining activity went by the front exit. Although it was tempting, not to mention faster, she knew better than to take the elevator.

The proposition of climbing eight flights of stairs to the tower suites with the air conditioning shut off was not one she relished, but there was no other way to safely get there now.

Opening the stairwell door, Marja started up the metallic stairs, moving as fast as she could. Praying it was fast enough.

He had trouble seeing.

Sweat kept dripping into his eyes, blurring his vision. Not to mention that there wasn't much light coming in. Lying under a hospital bed, trying to disarm a bomb, was not exactly a recommended way to pass a summer's afternoon.

The space was tight, but Kane couldn't risk raising the bed to allow himself more room. For all he knew, pressing the mechanical device could be the trigger.

Montgomery had just popped back into the room to tell him that the police had just taken the "orderly" with the laundry cart into custody. He'd had a cell phone on him, just like the man in the closet, and it had been confiscated, as well.

It should have made him feel a little safer, but it didn't. He'd been in this business long enough to know the deck was packed with wild cards. You thought you were playing a nice game of Blackjack only to discover that someone had gone and changed the rules on you and you were about to lose your shirt in a fast-paced game of Texas Hold 'Em.

He almost had it, he thought, blinking to get the sweat out of his eyes.

"Almost" was when people lost fingers and other important parts of their body.

So near and yet so far.

"Hey, Donnelly, the bomb squad's here!" Montgomery announced with relief. The agent stood in the doorway of the suite, as if that small distance from the bed made a difference in whether he lived or died if the bomb went off. "You can stop being a hero and give it over to the professionals. Hey, Donnelly, you hear me?" he asked, raising his voice when there was no response from under the bed.

Kane both felt and saw several pairs of black, rubber-soled boots coming toward him. For a second he felt as if he was glued in place by the perspiration pouring out of him. But then, he managed to wiggle out from beneath the bed.

"Just in time for clear-up," he said drily. Looking at the helmeted and well-padded man closest to him, he added, "It's disarmed and you're damn well welcome to it."

"You did it?" Montgomery cried in relieved wonder as he stepped back into the room.

"Yeah." The word was wrapped in overwhelmed weariness. Kane dragged the back of his wrist across his forehead, wiping off some of the perspiration. "I did it."

It was precisely at that moment that Marja ran into the room and launched herself at Kane. He had only enough time to open his arms and catch her as she wrapped her legs around his torso and sealed her mouth to his, kissing him over and over again.

"You're alive," she cried.

"Seems that way," he managed to mutter against her lips. Damn, but she felt good. He tightened his arms around her, letting himself just savor having her so close. A part of him had been fairly certain he wouldn't survive the half hour.

"Nice work, Donnelly," Montgomery commented. Hearing him, Kane had a hunch the other agent was talking more about the woman wrapped around his torso than his disarming the bomb.

Marja drew her head back. "Donnelly?" she echoed, looking at Kane in surprise. Now that the joy of seeing him alive had settled in, she had questions. Many.

In response to her quizzical repetition of his name, Kane shrugged carelessly, as if playing musical identities was no big thing.

"Miss, you're not supposed to be up here," a man who could have doubled as a storm trooper informed her, his voice echoing against the heavy-duty plastic guard extending from his helmet. He seemed ready to forcibly escort her off the floor.

Kane shifted so that he was between the man and Marja. "She's with me," Kane told him as Marja slid off his body and stood next to him. Despite what he'd just gone through, it was hard not reacting to that, Kane thought.

The head of the bomb squad had just entered the room. Looking at Kane, he asked, "And you are?"

Before he could answer, his handler materialized. One of the other agents must have called him, Kane realized.

"I'll explain everything, Sergeant," Frank promised,

flashing his credentials in such a way that only he and the sergeant could see. Putting his arm around the man's shoulders, he directed him off to the side.

"Can he explain it to me?" Marja asked, eyeing Kane. "Starting with who 'Donnelly' is?"

The drama was over. It was time for the credits to roll on the screen—the ones available for viewing. "I'm Donnelly," Kane told her.

She never took her eyes off him. "So who's Kane Dolan?"

His answer was far too noncommittal to suit her. "An orderly who worked here."

"Worked," she repeated. "As in past tense."

He was finished here. Taking her by the arm, he guided Marja out the door. There was clean-up to do and they would only be in the way. "Not needed here anymore."

She waited, but he didn't elaborate further. Big surprise.

"Do I get any more than that?" she finally asked once they were out in the corridor again. She could feel her temper getting the better of her.

Being closemouthed had never been difficult for him. But this time, it was different.

This time, everything was different.

"It's on a need-to-know basis." It was a line the Company had drummed into their heads over and over again.

Oh no, he wasn't about to get away with that. She'd been to hell and back in the space of a little more than an hour. She wanted more. Marja pulled her arm away from him and spun around to face him. "Well, I need to know. I *really* need to know." Her tone was almost fierce.

"Hey, Kane, don't wander off too far," Frank called after him, peering out of the suite into the hallway. "I need to debrief you."

Kane raised his hand over his head, signaling that he'd heard and would comply.

The term "debrief" brought a deliciously wicked image to her mind, but she squelched it. That kind of thinking, that kind of feeling, was what had gotten her in trouble to begin with.

As far as she knew, she was in love with a person who didn't exist. Who had never existed. It was a hell of a lonely feeling. How much of what he'd told her was a lie? Or was everything a lie? She felt like an idiot.

"Just who the hell are you?" she demanded. "I want an answer."

"Just someone with a job to do," he told her simply. "Like you."

"No, not like me," she countered angrily. "My life is an open book. Everyone knows my name, who my people are, where I come from. You're a damn giant walking question mark."

He never thought that anger could have a cute side— but on her, it did. It was hard for him not to smile. "I thought women liked mystery in a man."

"For about five minutes," she retorted. "Then we like some answers." And she wasn't about to back off or let him go until she had at least a few.

"Well—" Kane draped an arm over her shoulders as he steered her toward the elevator "—let's just say I'm not an orderly."

"I didn't ask you what you're not," Marja snapped.

"I asked you what you are. I just ran up eight flights of stairs to find out what happened to a man who apparently doesn't exist."

The elevator came. With his hand to her back, Kane gently pushed her in. Her blurted statement intrigued him. "You ran up eight flights of stairs?"

"Yes." The word fairly crackled with anger.

His eyes slid over her quickly as he pressed for the ground floor. "That explains why you're wetter than I am."

She shoved the wet bangs out of her eyes impatiently. "Well I'm really glad we solved that for you." Her voice fairly dripped of sarcasm. "Now why don't you—"

His voice cut through hers like a hot knife through butter. "Got another question for you. You said something earlier—"

She instantly knew where he was going, but that wasn't one of the things she wanted clarified. "I said a lot of things earlier."

"Just before you left," he continued as if she hadn't interrupted, "you said you loved me." His eyes on hers, Kane looked at her, waiting.

That had been a stupid thing to say, in light of what she now knew. Or, more to the point, didn't know. Marja shrugged, doing her best to seem indifferent, but anger got in her way, breaking through. "Stress of the moment. Didn't mean anything by it."

"Oh." He continued watching her. Ordinarily he would have shrugged it off. Retreated. But something held him in place. "Too bad."

"Did you want me to mean something by it?"

The elevator came to the ground floor. Again, as the doors opened, he guided her out. "Would my answer influence yours?"

The man really didn't have any experience in relationships, did he? "Hell, yes."

To her surprise, Kane shook his head. "Then I can't say."

She was getting a very bad headache, brought on more by this strange conversation than by what had transpired before it. "Why?" she demanded.

Now that the all-clear signal had been sounded, an inordinate number of law enforcement personnel as well as firefighters milled around on the ground floor, giving the area one last once-over before allowing staff and patients back into the hospital.

Moving slightly ahead of Marja, Kane forged a path for them. "Because then I won't know if you really do or not."

She stopped moving. When he turned to look at her, she snapped, "Okay, okay, okay, I love you," she admitted grudgingly. "But you don't have to worry. I'm not planning on stalking you."

His mouth curved. "You just ran up eight flights of stairs in an airless building that, as far as you knew, was all set to blow up, just to get to me."

He would throw that back in her face. Marja's jaw hardened. "You're an undercover lawyer, aren't you? You twist words for a living."

They'd reached the main entrance, but instead of going out, Kane suddenly pulled her over into the deserted X-ray facility. Pushing the door open, he drew her inside.

Now what? she wondered, startled.

"No," he told her, his expression deadly serious. "I'm a CIA agent. My name's Kane Donnelly and until you came along, I thought I was perfect for any job the Company threw my way because there was nothing in my life holding me back." His eyes washed over her, absorbing her. Loving her. "Nothing and no one that meant anything to me."

Her breath caught in her throat as she looked up at him. "And now?"

"And now," he told her honestly, "I'm not so sure."

For a moment she'd hoped... She really was an idiot, wasn't she? "Doesn't sound very positive."

His mouth curved just the slightest bit. "I'm positive I'm not sure."

She sighed. He was just giving her double-talk. "And what is that supposed to mean?"

Kane opened the door again, letting in the noise and commotion of the rest of the world. Taking her hand, he stepped out of the room. "I'll let you know when I work it out."

"I worked it out."

She almost hadn't answered the quick rap on her door when she'd heard it. It was a little after 11:00 p.m. and she was still trying to wind down from today, still trying to sort things out in her own head. Still trying to tell herself that she'd only gotten caught up in the momentum and didn't really feel what she knew to be true in her heart.

The bomb scare chaos at the hospital had finally

settled down. All the patients were back in their beds and the hospital routine was more or less back on schedule. But the events had brought a new sense of alarm to Patience Memorial so security, at least for the time being, was being beefed up and in some cases, doubled. Her father's firm had anted up every available body to do duty at P.M. until both the ambassador's daughter and the banking CEO were discharged. The hospital board convened on Monday to discuss a permanent hike in security personnel to ensure that something like this never happened again.

She hadn't seen Kane since they'd walked out of the X-ray facility together. Part of her was fairly certain that she would never see him again. That was what tonight was all about, convincing herself that she didn't care if she did or not.

And yet, here he was, making her heart skip all over again. Was he here with bad news, or good? She couldn't tell by his expression or even his tone. What made him a good operative made him a frustrating man to deal with to her.

"And what is it, exactly, that you've worked out?" she asked, closing the door.

He turned around to look at her. This afternoon had been one hell of a whirlwind. But throughout it all, he'd kept thinking of her. Whether he'd wanted to or not. Somewhere along the line, he'd decided that he wanted to. It had made up his mind for him.

"That I want you in my life."

"Really?" She wasn't going to take what he said at face value, wasn't going to just jump into his arms again—no matter how much she wanted to. He was going to have to spell things out for her.

"Then why do you look like someone who just resigned himself to a death sentence?" she challenged.

That made him laugh. "You might not have noticed this, but I'm not very expressive."

It was his laugh that put her at ease. He didn't laugh often and when he did, it didn't sound as relaxed as it did just now. "I did notice that. It's something you're going to have to work on."

He fit his hands around her waist, drawing her to him. "Does that mean you're going to try to change me?"

Oh damn, no matter how hard she tried, she couldn't talk herself out of him. Couldn't convince herself that she didn't care. Not even when every cell in her body had just launched into the *Hallelujah Chorus* at the mere touch of his hand.

"Just enough to let me know that I matter."

"You matter, Marja," he told her, his voice low, brushing along her skin. "You matter."

Just as she was about to say something, Kane kissed her, long and hard, stealing away not only her words but every single thought in her head.

Framing her face with his hands, he looked at her for a long moment. "I love you," he told her. "I didn't think I understood what those words meant, but now I do. I didn't care about being blown up, but I cared about you being blown up. I didn't want anything happening to you. If it had, I wouldn't have been able to continue."

"Continue," she echoed, shaking her head. "Not very good with romantic terms, are you?"

He couldn't argue with her. "At least you know I haven't had practice."

"Then you're going to need to practice," she told him, lacing her fingers around his neck. "With me. A lot." She punctuated each sentence with a kiss, each one lasting a little longer than the last.

No one could raise his body temperature faster than she could. It had been a hell of a long day, but peace was restored for another day, God was in His heaven and all was right with the world. Or so his handler liked to say. All he knew was that he didn't want to be any place but here. With her.

Kane glanced toward the rear of the apartment. "Are you alone?"

She nodded. "Tania's with Jesse." Bless her, she added silently.

"Good." His eyes on hers, he began to unbutton her shirt. "Oh, by the way…"

This was where he dropped his kind of bomb on her, she thought, bracing herself. "What?"

"How do you feel about marriage?"

She stopped his hands and looked at him, stunned. He wasn't saying what she thought he was saying—was he? "Are you taking a survey or asking me, personally?"

His smile went straight to her bones. The man really did have a very nice smile, she thought breathlessly. "I don't believe in surveys."

Wanting to scream yes, Marja took a deep breath instead. She wanted this to be absolutely clear with no room for misunderstanding. "I need a full sentence. Please."

For the first time in his life, he had no doubts about his decision. "Will you marry me?"

Oh God, she was going to cry. "And become Mrs. Secret Agent Man?"

"And become the best thing in my life."

She could feel emotions bursting inside of her like Fourth of July fireworks. "I stand corrected. You *can* say romantic things."

God, but he did love her. He hadn't realized how very much until just now. Until he was faced with the thought that she might say no. "Then it's yes?"

She laughed, raising herself up on her toes. "If you can't figure that out, you need to go back to Secret Agent school."

"Later." He gathered her closer to him. "I've got something more important to do right now."

"You bet you do," she said before she offered up her mouth to his.

* * * * *

Look for Marie Ferrarella's next
Silhouette Romantic Suspense
in October 2008.

THOROUGHBRED LEGACY
*The stakes are high when it comes to love,
horse racing, family secrets
and broken promises.*

*A new exciting Harlequin continuity series
coming soon!*
Led by New York Times *bestselling author*
Elizabeth Bevarly
FLIRTING WITH TROUBLE

Here's a preview!

THE DOOR CLOSED behind them, throwing them into darkness and leaving them utterly alone. And the next thing Daniel knew, he heard himself saying, "Marnie, I'm sorry about the way things turned out in Del Mar."

She said nothing at first, only strode across the room and stared out the window beside him. Although he couldn't see her well in the darkness—he still hadn't switched on a light…but then, neither had she—he imagined her expression was a little preoccupied, a little anxious, a little confused.

Finally, very softly, she said, "Are you?"

He nodded, then, worried she wouldn't be able to see the gesture, added, "Yeah. I am. I should have said goodbye to you."

"Yes, you should have."

Actually, he thought, there were a lot of things he should have done in Del Mar. He'd had *a lot* riding on the Pacific Classic, and even more on his entry, Little Joe, but after meeting Marnie, the Pacific Classic had been the last thing on Daniel's mind. His loss at Del Mar had pretty much ended his career before it had even begun, and he'd had to start all over again, rebuilding from nothing.

He simply had not then and did not now have room in his life for a woman as potent as Marnie Roberts. He was a horseman first and foremost. From the time he was a schoolboy, he'd known what he wanted to do with his life—be the best possible trainer he could be.

He had to make sure Marnie understood—and he understood, too—why things had ended the way they had eight years ago. He just wished he could find the words to do that. Hell, he wished he could find the *thoughts* to do that.

"You made me forget things, Marnie, things that I really needed to remember. And that scared the hell out of me. Little Joe should have won the Classic. He was by far the best horse entered in that race. But I didn't give him the attention he needed and deserved that week, because all I could think about was you. Hell, when I woke up that morning all I wanted to do was lie there and look at you, and then wake you up and make love to you again. If I hadn't left when I did—the way I did—I might still be lying there in that bed with you, thinking about nothing else."

"And would that be so terrible?" she asked.

"Of course not," he told her. "But that wasn't why I

was in Del Mar," he repeated. "I was in Del Mar to win a race. That was my job. And my work was the most important thing to me."

She said nothing for a moment, only studied his face in the darkness as if looking for the answer to a very important question. Finally she asked, "And what's the most important thing to you now, Daniel?"

Wasn't the answer to that obvious? "My work," he answered automatically.

She nodded slowly. "Of course," she said softly. "That is, after all, what you do best."

Her comment, too, puzzled him. She made it sound as if being good at what he did was a bad thing.

She bit her lip thoughtfully, her eyes fixed on his, glimmering in the scant moonlight that was filtering through the window. And damned if Daniel didn't find himself wanting to pull her into his arms and kiss her. But as much as it might have felt as if no time had passed since Del Mar, there were eight years between now and then. And eight years was a long time in the best of circumstances. For Daniel and Marnie, it was virtually a lifetime.

So Daniel turned and started for the door, then halted. He couldn't just walk away and leave things as they were, unsettled. He'd done that eight years ago and regretted it.

"It *was* good to see you again, Marnie," he said softly. And since he was being honest, he added, "I hope we see each other again."

She didn't say anything in response, only stood silhouetted against the window with her arms wrapped around her in a way that made him wonder whether she was doing it because she was cold, or if she just needed something—someone—to hold on to. In either case, Daniel understood. There was an emptiness clinging to him that he suspected would be there for a long time.

* * * * *

THOROUGHBRED LEGACY
coming soon wherever books are sold!

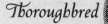

Thoroughbred *Legacy*

Launching in June 2008

A dramatic new 12-book continuity that embodies the American Dream.

Meet the Prestons, owners of Quest Stables, a successful horse-racing and breeding empire. But the lives, loves and reputations of this hardworking family are put at risk when a breeding scandal unfolds.

Flirting with Trouble

by *New York Times* bestselling author

ELIZABETH BEVARLY

Eight years ago, publicist Marnie Roberts spent seven days of bliss with Australian horse trainer Daniel Whittleson. But just as quickly, he disappeared. Now Marnie is heading to Australia to finally confront the man she's never been able to forget.

The stakes are high when it comes to love, horse racing, family secrets and broken promises.

A new exciting Harlequin continuity series coming soon!

www.eHarlequin.com

HT38984R

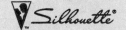

Cole's Red-Hot Pursuit

Cole Westmoreland is a man who gets what he
wants. And he wants independent and sultry
Patrina Forman! She resists him—until a Montana
blizzard traps them together. For three delicious
nights, Cole indulges Patrina with his brand of
seduction. When the sun comes out, Cole and
Patrina are left to wonder—will this be the end of
the passion that storms between them?

Look for

COLE'S RED-HOT PURSUIT

by USA TODAY bestselling author

BRENDA JACKSON

Available in June 2008 wherever you buy books.

Always Powerful, Passionate and Provocative.

REQUEST YOUR FREE BOOKS!

2 FREE NOVELS PLUS 2 FREE GIFTS!

Silhouette® Romantic

SUSPENSE

Sparked by Danger, Fueled by Passion!

YES! Please send me 2 FREE Silhouette® Romantic Suspense novels and my 2 FREE gifts (gifts are worth about $10). After receiving them, if I don't wish to receive any more books, I can return the shipping statement marked "cancel." If I don't cancel, I will receive 4 brand-new novels every month and be billed just $4.24 per book in the U.S. or $4.99 per book in Canada, plus 25¢ shipping and handling per book plus applicable taxes, if any*. That's a savings of at least 15% off the cover price! I understand that accepting the 2 free books and gifts places me under no obligation to buy anything. I can always return a shipment and cancel at any time. Even if I never buy another book from Silhouette, the two free books and gifts are mine to keep forever.

240 SDN EEX6 340 SDN EEYJ

Name	(PLEASE PRINT)	

Address		Apt. #

City	State/Prov.	Zip/Postal Code

Signature (if under 18, a parent or guardian must sign)

Mail to the **Silhouette Reader Service:**
IN U.S.A.: P.O. Box 1867, Buffalo, NY 14240-1867
IN CANADA: P.O. Box 609, Fort Erie, Ontario L2A 5X3

Not valid to current subscribers of Silhouette Romantic Suspense books.

Want to try two free books from another line?
Call 1-800-873-8635 or visit www.morefreebooks.com.

* Terms and prices subject to change without notice. N.Y. residents add applicable sales tax. Canadian residents will be charged applicable provincial taxes and GST. This offer is limited to one order per household. All orders subject to approval. Credit or debit balances in a customer's account(s) may be offset by any other outstanding balance owed by or to the customer. Please allow 4 to 6 weeks for delivery. Offer available while quantities last.

Your Privacy: Silhouette is committed to protecting your privacy. Our Privacy Policy is available online at www.eHarlequin.com or upon request from the Reader Service. From time to time we make our lists of customers available to reputable third parties who may have a product or service of interest to you. If you would prefer we not share your name and address, please check here. ☐

SRS08

Silhouette®

Romantic
SUSPENSE

**Sparked by Danger,
Fueled by Passion.**

Seduction Summer:
Seduction in the sand…and a killer on the beach.

*Silhouette Romantic Suspense invites you to the hottest
summer yet with three connected stories from some
of our steamiest storytellers! Get ready for…*

Killer Temptation
by **Nina Bruhns;**
a millionaire this tempting is worth a little danger.

Killer Passion
by **Sheri WhiteFeather;**
an FBI profiler's forbidden passion incites a
killer's rage,

and

Killer Affair
by **Cindy Dees;**
this affair with a mystery man is to die for.

Look for

KILLER TEMPTATION by Nina Bruhns in June 2008
KILLER PASSION by Sheri WhiteFeather in July 2008
and
KILLER AFFAIR by Cindy Dees in August 2008.

Available wherever you buy books!

Visit Silhouette Books at www.eHarlequin.com

SRS27586

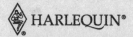

Silhouette®
Romantic
SUSPENSE

COMING NEXT MONTH

#1515 PROTECTING HIS WITNESS—Marie Ferrarella
Cavanaugh Justice
Having left medicine, Krystle Maller is shocked to find a man lying unconscious on her doorstep. She's been in hiding from the mob since witnessing a murder. She fears her discovery might get her—or him—killed, yet she treats her handsome patient. While a gunshot wound may slow him down, undercover cop Zack McIntyre is skilled at protecting the innocent. And he certainly won't let Krystle handle a dangerous threat on her own....

#1516 KILLER TEMPTATION—Nina Bruhns
Seduction Summer
Finding a dead man at the start of her dream job is Zoe Conrad's worst nightmare. But when the man proves to be very much alive—plus charming, filthy rich and sexy as all get out—Zoe knows she's in even more trouble. Giving in to Sean Guthrie's incendiary seduction could be her worst mistake yet. Because while Sean claims to know nothing about the serial killer who's stalking couples on the beach, local authorities have their eyes on Sean and Zoe…and so might a murderer.

#1517 SAFE WITH A STRANGER—Linda Conrad
The Safekeepers
On the run with nowhere to hide, Clare Chandler would stop at nothing to protect her child. Army Ranger Josh Ryan has spent his life hiding from his true identity and relates to the way Clare keeps herself guarded when he rescues her and her son from her ex's henchmen. In order to help them, however, he must face his family and the truth of who he really is…while withstanding his fiery attraction to Clare.

#1518 DANGEROUS TO THE TOUCH—Jill Sorenson
Homicide detective Marc Cruz doesn't care for second-rate con artists—especially those claiming they have psychic powers and a lead on his serial-killer case. Although Marc intends to expose Sidney Morrow for the hoax she is, her impressions—about the investigation and his attraction to her—are proving all too true.

SRSCNM0508